In the
Bleak
Midwinter

❄ ❄ ❄

Catherine Ritch Guess

To Starla,
Many winter
wonderlands of
blessing !

Catherine Ritch Guess
August 29, 2003.

CRM BOOKS

CRM, P.O. Box 365
Paw Creek, NC 28130
www.ciridmus.com

Publisher's Cataloging-in-Publication
(*Provided by Quality Books, Inc.*)

Guess, Catherine Ritch.
    In the bleak midwinter / Catherine Ritch Guess. --
1st ed.
    p. cm. -- (Shooting star series ; 1)
    LCCN: 2002094568
    ISBN: 0-9713534-3-3

    1. Concord(N.C.)--Fiction. 2. Band music--Fiction.
3. Wesley, John, 1703-1791--Fiction. 4. Jarrett, Dale,
1956---Fiction. 5. Christmas stories. I. Title.

PS3557.U34385I68 2003   813'.6
                              QBI03-700308

To

Sherri Brown

the closest thing
to a sister
I ever had

Merry Christmas,
2003

Special Thanks

to Dale A. Jarrett, Nascar driver, and to Kirk Stump, General Manager of Dale Jarrett Ford, Indian Trail, NC, for their support and permission to use real names in this book, and its sequel, *There's a Song in the Air*. An added word of appreciation goes to James Gaither, Mr. Jarrett's business manager, for his gracious assistance in working out all the necessary details.

And most especially, thank you for making a difference in the lives of so many through the Dale Jarrett Foundation.

Acknowledgments

To the Wesley Ringers of Pleasant Grove UMC, Charlotte, NC -the finest bell choir I ever conducted. Your peals of *In the Bleak Midwinter* from the balcony continually played through my mind as I wrote this book.

To RuthEllen Busbee-Boerman, whose painting, *The Stayin' Place*, provided the perfect setting and cover for the story already in my head.

To Jerry DeCeglio, who once again took the idea in my head and made it work on the cover. Many thanks!

To Kip Burke, my editor, for his continual encouragement, advice and friendship

To my former students, the staff, and administration of Cabarrus Academy, Concord, NC, who made teaching a most rewarding experience for me. As I penned this Christmas novel, the memory of your faces and voices kept my hands in motion on the computer keyboard.

To Richard Snyder, headmaster at Cabarrus Academy (now Cannon School), who trusted my expertise probably more times than he should have

To Gay Roberts, of Cabarrus Academy, a wonderful mentor. Every teacher should be so fortunate as to work with such a caring and dedicated person.

To Milton and Myrtle Cornette, whose beach house provided the perfect retreat for me to write this novel

To Gary and Cindy Hoback, whose bed and breakfast - Wolf Creek Farm in VA - provided the therapeutic quiet I needed to get through the final draft and bluelines

To Bill and Nancy Benfield who, through their never-ending examples of unconditional love for others, have taught me more about benevolence and good will than anyone I know

To Dr. Daniel Howard, Dr. Toni Evans, Dr. Robert Yavorski, Jim Gordon - PA, and Nella Linker - *nurse extraordinaire*, whose medical expertise led to a miraculous recovery; to my family and friends whose daily prayers helped me keep my bright spirit and positive attitude, allowing me to win my battle with dermatomyositis; and especially to my mom, Corene Ritch, who had to help me learn to walk, talk, eat, and get dressed all over again. Without all of you, this book would be forever lost in the computer. Thank you for helping me not only survive, but for making a winter wonderland out of my bleak midwinter.

But most especially, to Rob Bratton, Reed Fabek, Ford Koch, Yorke Pharr, Jamie Purser and Jason Sanderbeck - You are the six whose perfectly pitched voices and impeccable enunciation on *Gesu Bambino* stills inspires me after all these years - ***obviously***.

In the
Bleak
Midwinter

CHAPTER 1

Celia Brinkley scanned the stage again carefully, glancing over her long to-do list one last time before she locked the door of the auditorium. The concert grand piano from her classroom had been carefully rolled in for the evening's performance, the first musical program at the new location of Tillman Academy. At any other time, this veteran music teacher would have sat down and let her long, thin fingers glide across the eighty-eight keys stretching out before her, letting their sounds elevate her soul to a higher realm.

Instead, she reached up and tucked her shoulder length, dark-brunette strands behind her ears, a habit she caught herself doing when something was amiss.

Any music or drama teacher in her right mind would be thrilled at having an auditorium like this at her disposal. And quite satisfactory to Celia it was, for she had been granted the privilege of suggesting specifications to the architect for its design. That was one time she had been grateful for the many musicals and concerts she had planned, written and directed for the school, not to mention being in charge of the weekly assemblies when she brought in special guests. Otherwise, she wouldn't have been allowed the opportunity of exercising her expertise.

The deep purple velvet of the stage curtain, by itself, demanded the attention of anyone who happened to be in the huge facility. Combined with the appropriate latest technology in lighting for the evening's concert, it had the capability of changing the tone of the room from the showy, regal glitz of the opening *We Need a Little Christmas* to the warm, yet hefty, royal dominance of *Masters in This Hall*. Celia was well aware that the plush theater-style seats, with a varying shade of the same purple hue as the curtain, might be a detriment to the acoustics. But hopefully the wooden floor of the huge stage, and the circular brick walls that outlined the auditorium, would reverberate the sound of the children's voices enough that their hard work would not have been in vain.

There was no other school in the area with a piano that compared to the Bösendorfer that had been donated in memory of one of her former students who, as a college student, had been killed in a car accident. The girl's father, a local surgeon, had offered the contribution at the time the school's building program was announced. He wanted to give the music teacher time to find an instrument that was as fair as his flower that had perished. Celia was even flown to Austria to select just the right piano before it ever left the factory.

She never once questioned the judgment of that extravagance, for she knew it filled a giant void for the generous doctor and his wife. And as badly as Celia hated to admit it, it gave a sense of prominence to the couple at the country club, and around the small town of Tillman, North Carolina.

With that thought, Celia Brinkley stopped in place. That was what had bothered her time and time again throughout her years of teaching. She had the good fortune of working in a private facility, where there were many benefactors. There was never a need where she was concerned. Her excellent track record had brought national attention to the school by her demand as an instructor for various music and drama seminars. The annual had been dedicated to her one year in honor of her fine programs, her expertise, and her dedication. For all of her hard work and devotion, the students' families had been quick to show their appreciation through various monetary gifts to the music department.

Nevertheless, she knew that Uncle Sam and prestige were the reasons for many of the gifts to the school, rather than heartfelt generosity. Yet, Celia knew she couldn't condemn the benefactors, for she was in the same boat. She had indeed poured herself into her job over the years, a fact that played a large part in the success of her classes and programs, but a part of it had served as a selfish escape since she had no husband or children to demand any of her attention. Her devotion and commitment were, in effect, a distraction from the loneliness.

Suddenly, Celia was aware of the lesson that she wanted to bestow on her students before she left them. A lesson that conveyed that in order to give a gift, *to really give it from the heart*, one must truly make a sacrifice.

The musician was gratified that she'd been able to teach her students many lessons through all the musicals and various field trips over the years. She was the teacher who guided her students on international tours, giving them opportunities to sing in world-renowned cathedrals, and taking them to hidden catacombs to study the mysteries of history. To Celia, music was more than an artistic form. It was also an outlet to teach her students about every possible subject.

As she stood there, giving the room a last once-over before its debut concert, it became evident that an extremely creative strategy was needed in order to teach her students one of the most valuable lessons they would ever learn.

I'd better tackle that project after *the concert this evening,* she reasoned, pulling herself back to the purpose of the checklist in her hand.

The risers were all in place, the tree was professionally decorated, props were in the appropriate places, all the rhythm and Orff instruments, with their mallets, had been brought in, and the bell tables were up and the bells newly polished. Programs were placed at each entrance, ready for the hostesses. Celia's music was all in order on the piano, complete with instructions on how to get from one piece to another. She shook her head, wondering why she even bothered with that formality. By this point in the game, she had every detail, as well as every word and note, memorized.

She closed the door and turned out the lights as she exited the auditorium and headed for her classroom. Celia tried to think on the positive side as she walked down the hallway, hoping to get her emotional state in gear for the upcoming evening. Yes, by measure of the standard school auditorium, this one far surpassed the mark. And by the standard of the average school program, her students again far surpassed the mark. Many of her students not only took private lessons, but from the best orchestra players of the nearest symphony, thirty miles away in Charlotte.

Nothing was too good for her students. The caliber of wealth of their families ranged from the old money of a worldwide industrial tycoon to the nouveau riche of the team crew chief of a winning Nascar driver.

She laughed. Had it not been for the crew chief's money, and all that the school could accomplish with the bucks that came with his child's enrollment, Celia wondered if the volunteer mothers would have been so quick to welcome his wife into their social arena. More likely, they would have treated her with the same attitude they treated the fans of the sport who came into town each spring and fall.

Celia stopped her wandering mind, for she had neither the desire nor the energy to exert any more effort here, including taking herself to a loftier place through the music of the piano. Instead, she was going home to take a nap, hoping to get herself revved up before she hit the first note of the annual Christmas concert.

Perhaps I should call the crew chief of the local Nascar driver instead of the trusted doctor next time I feel under the weather. He obviously knows how to get things up and run-

ning. Celia chuckled, going out the door, wishing there was an instant remedy for her sudden need of an adrenalin rush before the demanding evening facing her.

The wise teacher was aware of her problem. It was typical among many of her peers, who had also taught for a number of years. *Burn-out.* That point of wondering whether you were making a difference, whether another career would allow you to do more for others, or whether you even cared anymore.

What bothered Celia the most was the fact that her name stood for the patron saint of music, a point she was sure was not on the list of reasons for her mother adorning her with that given name. And now, here she was, having emphatically vowed she would never reach this point of complacency with her music, stuck at its summit – spinning her gears.

Now I know it's time to call the crew chief. Between spinning gears and burn-out, - which have to be akin to blow-outs and spin-outs - *he has to have some kind of advice to move me past this rut!*

Celia knew her silly thoughts most definitely indicated that it was time for a nap before the concert. But then, she was aware she had to do something to keep her wits about her, for "the show must go on."

She felt sure that when it came time for contract renewals in February, hers would not get turned back in to Dr. Lacey, the headmaster of Tillman's fine academy. And she knew he would come to her, reason with her, offer her more money, paint a pretty picture, and she might be tempted to stick it out, like the others who had battled this demon of the realistic working world.

Celia pictured the scenario in her mind. George Lacey would come by her office during one of her planning breaks, dressed in his wrinkle-free navy slacks, camel-colored sports coat and dark-brown loafers, his peppering silver and black hair all in place and adding to his look of distinction.

His looks could have easily won him a seat in a CEO chair of any organization, but he preferred to spend his days out on the field coaching, or in the classrooms encouraging his students. There was not a time the music teacher could remember when the look of love and concern for "his children" was not written all over his face. And the students recognized that fact, too, for their actions visibly spoke of a confidence they felt in him, yet they regarded him with full respect.

So, Celia mused, *in effect he is a CEO. He sits in his big plush office and governs over the teachers – his Board of Directors – and the students.*

She hoped she would be armed and ready when their conference came, for the list of pros at Tillman Academy made it easy to paint a pretty picture – especially for one in an artistic field.

Amusingly, Celia thought that perhaps she

should apply with her college alma mater to teach a class on burn-out, and how to prevent it. She had in no way been prepared to face it. In fact, she had left school with the same idealistic views as everyone else who got sent out into the world to "change it for the better."

This is not helping me prepare for tonight's concert, she scolded herself, aggravated that she was letting her mind again wander when it should be focusing on the evening ahead. She recognized that as another personal habit that raised its ugly head when something was bothering her – something that her subconscious was consciously trying to avoid.

There was one last item that Celia had to take care of before she left for the afternoon. She had purposely waited until most of the teachers and students left to finish her list. The music teacher combed the hallways looking for Donnie Little, the school's custodian. Of course, he was in the last building she entered, rearranging tables for the luncheon to be given for the teachers and administration the next day by the volunteers. It seemed his work never ended, yet she had not once seen him be cross, or refuse to do a task that didn't even remotely fall into his job description.

Celia had watched as others left him notes, or lists of menial chores, seldom taking the time to speak to him. And she watched him carry out his duties, always with a smile. She also noticed that he walked through the hallways with his head lowered most of the time, a habit that she suspected came from not wanting to be hurt by the fact that few people ever regarded him – even with a simple "hello" - be it teachers or students.

She had invited Donnie into her classroom recently for the students to sing *Happy Birthday* to him. They were not supposed to have unauthorized parties, but she used the class period as a study on the births of several familiar children's songs, thereby bringing in cupcakes and punch. The students loved the class, and it gave her an opportunity to show the custodian that he was loved and appreciated. Celia also hoped that it would encourage the students to speak to him in the hallways.

Her Theories of Education professor had taught her a long time ago that the two most important figures on the school staff were the secretary and the custodian. For that reason, Celia made a point of always speaking to Donnie, and giving him a big smile that matched the one he gave her each morning. She had anonymously left desserts in his box throughout the year. And she made sure she thanked him profusely before and after every program, for which he graciously helped her set up and clear the stage and auditorium.

That's why she had brought him a spiral-sliced ham for Christmas. She had opted to give it to him personally so that hopefully he would see it was a gift of appreciation rather than a hand-out for some person to be pitied.

He turned his head and nodded at her, flashing the usual smile that appeared when he saw her. His simple acknowledgement of her presence made Celia glad for her decision.

"Donnie, do you have a spare minute to come down to my room?"

"Yes, Miss Brinkley. Just let me move these last four tables."

"Take your time," she responded, noting how fortunate the school was to have someone like him in this role.

Celia wished she could tell him to call her by her first name, and lose the title, but she knew that was strictly against school policy. All the teachers and administration were expected to call the other staff members by their appropriate title and surname as a fitting example for the students. *All the staff, that is, except Donnie*, she caught herself. And that was probably because he was generally ignored as he made his way through the hallways.

He followed her to her classroom, as if it were the respectful thing to do. She made small talk along the way, impressed by the vocabulary of this otherwise quiet man. Celia went to her storage room and brought

out the large box she had taken from the lounge's re-
frigerator minutes earlier.

"Here, Donnie. Merry Christmas. Please accept
this as a small token of appreciation for all you do for
me around this place."

"Oh, Miss Brinkley, I can't take this. What I do
for you is my job."

"Yes, I know that. But your job does *not* include
all the moving of instruments and the extra preparations for my programs. And it most certainly does *not*
say that "you must be pleasant at all times" in your job
description. So for those things, please know that it
makes me feel partially better to be able to offer you
this tiny expression of gratitude."

"Thank you. Thank you very much, Miss
Brinkley," he said, tipping his head. "My grandmaw
always taught me never to look a gift horse in the
mouth."

Celia loved the rural dialect and polite Southern
manners that had probably been passed down by that
grandmaw. And she highly suspected that same
grandmaw was the person who taught Donnie not to
accept charity.

She looked at him, seeing beneath the outward
appearance that most of the other faculty saw. His light
brown hair was still cut in a sixties' style, hanging about
his collar, with bangs nearly covering his thick eyebrows.

Donnie's long-sleeved plaid shirt of golds and browns looked as if it might only survive a couple more runs through the washing machine, and his bell-bottomed jeans were not a fashion statement, but ones that had surely been picked up at a local thrift store. The observant teacher made a note to speak to the headmaster about uniforms for this employee.

"What time do you plan to unlock the auditorium this evening?" Celia asked.

"I'll be here shortly after six. I have to go home for a few minutes to pick up something, then I'll be right back."

The music teacher couldn't help but notice how this man beamed as he spoke to her, proud of his responsibility in preparation for the arrival of all the students and their guests. Had she not known better, she would have thought he was a main stage performer given his enthusiasm about his task.

"Good, I'll be back shortly after that, also. But be sure you get a bite of supper first. Perhaps this will make that a little easier, " she said, tapping on the box containing the ham.

He exited the room, a broad smile on his face. Until that moment, Celia had never thought about whether Donnie had a wife or a family at home. She hoped that he had someone with whom to share his gift, providing for him a meaningful opportunity, too.

Leaving all thoughts of the upcoming evening's program in the auditorium, Celia left the school for the afternoon. She was determined to have a quiet, relaxing nap, and a small bite before the concert, concluding that age was the main factor contributing to her current lack of energy.

Tuesday evening once again. The teacher mentally noted how all the concerts were held on a Tuesday evening, with Wednesday being the last day of school before Christmas vacation. It had become a long-standing tradition at Tillman Academy. And it had also become a long-standing tradition for Celia to have the other two days before the weekend to unwind, do whatever shopping was still necessary, and relax before sharing the holiday season with her parents and sister.

This year will be the same, Celia muttered to herself as she made the turn out of the long, rolling driveway of the school, ready for the break.

CHAPTER 2

As a rule, Celia longed for someone to come and share in the afterglow of the evening following one of her performances. The small talk of company seemed to set the tone as her body let itself drift back to normal – physically, mentally and emotionally – following the adrenalin rush that accompanied the natural high for an artist. Yet, as she got dressed this evening, she breathed a sigh of relief that she would be returning to the comfort of her quiet home in the historic district - *alone*.

She had already laid her pink chenille robe on the bed, and placed a new book she had been longing to read on the chair in front of the gas logs in the formal living room. Celia had the table set "for one" beside the footed flame-stitched St. Anne's chair, sure that she would come home with the usual array of delectable sensations that swamped her at this festive season.

And if she was correct in her assumption, she would also have received festive napkins and paper dinnerware on which to serve herself when she returned, along with a gourmet assortment of flavored hot chocolates.

Oh well, it's nice to be pampered in some ways, she sighed, taking one of her many formal gowns from the closet. As much as she loved getting dressed up for black-tie events, she was in no mood for the gala attire of the evening. Because of that, Celia chose her most exquisite black silk dress, with gold dangling beads and black shiny bangles covering the entire bodice and sleeves. She was sure that the shimmering reflections from all the new stage lighting, bouncing off her every move, would add to the sparkle of the evening. And the fullness of the taffeta skirt, reminiscent of a Ginger Rodgers era, would allow her to make a grand entrance, with the hem flowing gracefully around her ankles as she walked across the stage to the piano.

The only thing missing will be Fred Astaire and his

top hat! she laughed, glad something was getting her mind into a humored mood.

Her tall, slender shape gave her the appearance of a ballroom dancer as she glided across the floor, watching the layers of the black skirt sweep around the room. As she fastened the hook at the nape of her neck, letting the long slit that revealed her back take shape, Celia thought about all the children getting dressed for the evening's event.

Let's see, she figured, doing a quick calculation in her head, *there are seven hundred children singing in tonight's concert. I know most of their mothers shop at the exclusive boutique in town, so a full outfit will cost at least two or three hundred dollars. Heaven forbid that one of them would wear a hand-me-down from an older brother or sister.*

And there, ladies and gentlemen, we have precisely proven my point, Celia surmised, reflecting on her thought from earlier in the day about showing off to the other members of the social circle. *The first item on my agenda for the New Year will be to teach the children about priorities in life. I wonder how many of them have ever heard the story of the widow's mite?*

She took one last look in the mirror, saying a short prayer of thanks that she had been blessed with dark eyes that still sparkled with the same luster as her hair. Dressed in her concert attire, Celia noted that her features were perfect for this role. It must have been her destiny to be a performer who would spend much of her time donned in black.

CHAPTER 3

The perceptive music teacher had been right in her earlier assessment about the children's clothing. As she strolled from classroom to classroom, speaking to her students and giving them last-minute instructions, she noted that they were dressed only in the finest Christmas outfits that money could buy. It amazed her that with seven hundred students, none of them were dressed alike, not even the sets of twins, or the triplets.

Obviously the owner of the boutique has learned not

to let such a social disgrace happen!

Seeing the children so finely dressed, and more impressively, anxious to do everything she asked of them, truly tugged at Celia's heartstrings. She sincerely loved her job, *and* the students. Her enthusiasm showed in the performances through the hard work of the boys and girls who obviously went to great lengths to please their music teacher.

She walked into the fourth grade pod, hugging the students as they came running up to greet her, showering her with gifts, their eyes full of wonder and curiosity at what tidbit of musical knowledge their mentor would give them this night. *And what a surprise they will get in class tomorrow for their excellent performance!* Celia loved this group. They had been under her tutorage long enough to develop a true appreciation of the renowned composers and their music. And they knew precisely what their teacher expected of them regarding proper performance etiquette and behavior. This was the group that had finally matured into keeping their eyes totally focused on her as she directed them.

Celia felt especially close to this particular grade level. When one of their classes had done book reports on biographies earlier in the year, every single student had chosen a composer for their person of note. That fourth grade's teacher had sent Celia a memo and asked what magical things were going on in her classroom.

Just as she had shown her appreciation to Donnie earlier in the day, now parents and children were doing the same for her. Celia felt pleasantly humbled as she walked down hall after hall and looked into the faces of her students. Even the children who were not particularly musical were primed and ready for their big night, if only out of respect for the woman they knew loved them. Her efforts of finding special jobs for her "unmusical" subjects had paid off. Everyone would be able to go home, all of them "stars" in their own right, after a remarkable performance, and every parent could be proud of their child, *and the outfit.*

As she walked down the last hallway, Celia's emotional level had risen to match that of her students. She still felt a bit alarmed, for always before it had been *her* who had fed *them* with her energy.

No matter, she reasoned, *the show will go on, and I'll be rearing and ready to go by the time all the classes have made their grand entrance.*

From the moment the students hauled in the holly for *We Need a Little Christmas,* placing candles in the windows and acting out the lyrics of the opening number in carefully staged movements, Celia felt her own spirit bouncing off the wall with those of the children. The flashes of cameras, belonging to proud parents, added a fireworks effect to the brightness in the air already being created by the young voices.

Celia was glad she had incorporated strings, bells and flutes into the second piece. By the time that one was completed, she was floating in her normal lofty altitude for such an event, and was ready to put it on cruise control for the remainder of the concert. She had made up her mind before she got here not to let her lack of enthusiasm show to her students or their parents. And she certainly had no intention of letting it affect the performance of all these children who had worked so hard during class time.

The kindergarteners tickled her with delight as they sang about Santa with great excitement. Their thrill was equally matched by the first and second graders who set a winter-time scene with their medley of snow songs. Her third and fourth graders played superbly on their *Pastorale* from Handel's <u>Messiah</u> written especially for their orchestra of recorders and Orff instruments.

She allowed herself to back off and become completely enthralled in the sounds coming from the voices and instruments, something she had never done during a live performance. It dawned on her that she was actually *not* the one in charge here, for it was *rather* the One who had blessed her and all these children with their talents.

Celia watched as her ballet students soared through the air during a handbell and flute medley from *The Nutcracker,* followed by three liturgical dancers from her middle school class who enhanced the chorale of *Jesu, Joy of Man's Desiring* with their artistic interpretation.

As she became a part of what was happening through the eyes and voices of her students, she was as mesmerized as the parents who were spellbound by the talents and professionalism of these young performers. When it came time for the final segment of the concert, and her elite boys' ensemble stepped forward, Celia held her breath, praying that their perfectly pitched voices and their impeccable enunciation of the Latin text would be unmatched, even by the angels in heaven.

The teacher gazed intently at these fourth and fifth graders - six boys who had excelled in their classes in every way - and who had been granted voices that were astounding for their ages. Her skill had combined their individual gifts into an ensemble that she would have put up against any boys' choir anywhere in the world.

They stood there, in their handsome blazers and Christmas ties, ready to become her instrument as she conducted them through *Gesu Bambino.* From the very first note, it became apparent that the entire audience was captivated, and transported to an emotional high. There was not a sound throughout the entire auditorium except the six boys' purest of voices, and the violin accompanying their teacher on the piano.

As they grew into the final crescendo near the end of the piece, Celia heard a baby's low cry. Tears formed in her eyes as she realized that she had been transformed, along with the rest of the audience.

She looked at the glow of candles in the windows, and the soft lighting on the deep purple stage curtain that gave it a dominating effect over the entire room. The enormous tree, given by the founding family of the school, twinkled with tiny, clear lights that were nowhere comparable to the sparkle in the eyes of the seven hundred boys and girls assembled on the stage and the risers.

Celia closed her eyes, basking in the emotion of the moment. She had heard the story of John Wesley, the founder of Methodism, describing his experience of feeling "strangely warmed." The music teacher knew exactly how he must have felt, for at that precise moment, she envisioned all of heaven opening, and the angels reaching out to join the voices and the instruments of her students. Knowing the rest of her life would be touched by that mystical moment, she wondered if anyone besides her was moved to the point of hearing a baby's cry during the singing of the carol.

The overcome teacher decided that her creative imagination had kicked into gear, allowing her to literally see and hear the nativity scene through the boys' voices. She dismissed the feeling as a moment of overwhelming emotion, brought on by the divinely acoustical effect of the auditorium matched by its visual highlights, yet conflicted by her struggle of feeling the syndrome of burn-out, ushered in with great fury, earlier in the day.

Her thoughts turned to the words of Christina Rosetti's poem, *In the Bleak Midwinter*, as she played soft chords behind the children's voices. The climax of the concert, planned to send chills down the spine of each person in the audience, was when one of the girls sang the final stanza a cappella, asking simply, "What can I give him, poor as I am? If I were a shepherd, I would bring a lamb. If I were a Wise Man, I would do my part, But what I can I give Him, give Him my heart."

The innocence of the girl's voice flawlessly hitting the pitches of the simple melody of the carol accomplished exactly what Celia had hoped for – a moment of silence that caused one to look into the depths of their own soul to see what gift they had for the Messiah. Combined with the emotion of the preceding *Gesu Bambino*, the music teacher was most definitely ready for the children to bounce into the last piece with the rollicking rhythm of "The snow lay on the ground, the stars shone bright, when Christ the Lord was born on Christmas night."

All of the students joined their voices as the boys' ensemble led that most joyous and impressive arrangement of *Venite Adoramus* for the finale of the performance that brought everyone to their feet in thunderous applause and a standing ovation. The audience's response was nothing new, but the sound literally rang through the new auditorium, giving it the same effect as having several thousand fans in a huge concert hall.

Celia was thrilled for her students, as she imagined this being the last Christmas she would ever share her abilities with them. Leaving them would be hard, especially after such an awesome display of their talents, but still she wondered if she had not reached her climax here, an indication that she should move on to a new assignment. *Maybe even to a job out of the teaching field – at least of children.* She forgot this thought for the time being, and stood to take a bow, then held out her hand for the students to do the same.

How wonderful they are.

She could see Dr. Lacey's satisfaction as he moved forward to publicly thank her for the extremely hard work of herself and the students, and present her with the annual bouquet of red roses.

Too bad I'm leaving. I'd have another raise wrapped up and in the bag.

After another round of thunderous applause, and the presentation of several dozens of red roses from various classes, Celia posed for what seemed hundreds of pictures by proud parents, with her arms around their children. One by one, parents and students brought her presents too beautifully wrapped to open. She, in turn, reminded the students to be sure to retrieve their individual red carnations, her gift to them, before they went home.

When the last person had exited the building, she sat down again briefly at the piano and thought about the unusual experience she had during the boys' performance. Celia wondered whether it had been a divine message telling her to stay with this job, or an expression of a job well done for many years of faithful service. *Or if it was merely my imagination and love of music getting the best of me.*

As she closed her eyes and mentally heard an encore of the *Gesu Bambino*, she once again heard the faintest sound of a baby far off in the distance. She opened her eyes and looked around in the silence of the room, trying to make some sense out of what she had just heard.

Oh well, I guess I tried a little too hard to recreate the effect of the musical moment.

She boxed up the assortment of gifts she had been given by the students. Celia laughed to herself, thinking how she could probably go through these boxes and gift bags and find everything she needed for her own Christmas list. They were already wrapped in incredibly gorgeous packages, just waiting to be opened.

As she walked through the parking lot to pull her car up to where she could load all of the presents, wondering how many of them would eventually find themselves in the church's spring rummage sale, Celia found herself wishing Donnie were nearby to help her. It was going to take several trips to get all of her stash.

I guess I'm no better than all the others who are always looking for him only when they need help.

Suddenly she felt ashamed at her thought, hoping that Donnie didn't perceive her to be taking advantage. Celia remembered her mission from a previous afternoon, of finding a way for the students to learn to appreciate this man for his role in keeping the school in fine order, and for his personal cheerful disposition. Thinking of him now made her more determined to find a way to casually let that happen once the students were back for the New Year.

She busied herself gathering all the boxes and gift bags, filling the trunk and the back seat of her car, thinking, as every year, that she was going to have to get a bigger house just to find a place for all her gifts. The teacher had found herself wishing, the past couple of years, that students would not give her presents, but rather, would make a charitable contribution to some organization for needy children. By the time she neared the last of her loads, she had decided to make that recommendation at the next faculty meeting.

Celia had carefully placed all the freshly made goodies in the front seat so they would be easily accessible when she got home. She could already feel herself stretched out in front of the fireplace, her body wrapped in the warmth of her chenille robe, and taste the delectable sweets, her reward for the evening.

That thought made her step a little quicker as she picked up the last armload of presents. As she walked toward the back door, wondering whether to turn out the lights or let Donnie do it, she heard a baby's low cry again.

Celia stopped dead in her tracks. Her ears were not deceiving her this time. Nor was her mind swayed by the soft glow of lights against the regal stage curtain, or the perfectly pitched voices. She definitely heard a baby crying.

A chilling tingle ran up her spine as she gently placed the presents in a chair. *Should I call 911? Should I look for Donnie?* All Celia knew was that she had to do something, but she had no idea as to what.

She listened intently, trying to decide on the location of the sound. It seemed to be more audible near the vents. Celia moved back to where the piano was to see if there was a vent there, also.

Just as I figured! she noted, spying three vents in the floor right in front of the stage.

The cry was so weak that it was surely coming from a newborn infant. Either that, or it was a baby that had been abandoned, and had become extremely weak. Celia decided that she had to do something immediately, and then call for help.

As she made her way down the steps to the boiler room, she wondered whether she would even be able to get into it. Surely she could find Donnie if need be, and get him to unlock the door. Thoughts of what could happen to her should have been running through her head, but all she could think about was a small abandoned child, each second counting in its struggle for life.

Why did I have to tell Dr. Lacey I would be fine when he asked if I wanted him to stay until I left? Next time, Celia Brinkley, don't be so blamed independent!

The lights were off in the hallway when she reached the bottom of the stairs. Wishing she had a flashlight, she fumbled her hands along the wall until she found the light switches.

Sure enough, she heard the faint sound of a baby's whimper coming from inside the boiler room. Celia tiptoed closer, not wanting to be heard should there be any danger, hoping the hall lights had not been visible from the hiding place of whoever was in the room with the baby – *if there is anyone else.*

Celia thought of tapping lightly on the door, but determined the best thing to do was fling it open, hopefully surprising the culprit, should there be anyone there. She turned the knob quickly and shoved against the door, almost afraid to look inside.

What she saw was the school's custodian, crouched on one knee, looking at a baby that lay cradled on the lap of a tiny woman.

"Donnie, is everything okay?" she asked, grateful that he had already found the person hiding with the newborn infant, and that she didn't have to face this situation alone. Her respect for him rose several more notches at his efficient care for the facility. *And its inhabitants!*

Then she noticed the change of expression on his face as a look of simple shame showed his visual apology for being found here.

"Everything is fine, Miss Brinkley. This is my wife, Anna, and our new baby, Bobby." The usual smile was not evident as he lowered his head. "There was no heat at our house, so I brought them here to stay warm during the concert."

The mother nodded humbly. "The baby really enjoyed the music. We could hear the children's voices so clearly through the vents. They sang him to sleep with their beautiful songs."

"What are you going to do now?" Celia questioned the custodian.

"We'll go back to our house as soon as I lock up."

"Will the heat be back on?" the teacher asked, full of concern.

The couple looked at each other, neither wanting to speak.

Celia could tell there was something amiss here. "Why don't you come to my house and stay the evening? There's plenty of room, and you would all be most comfortable."

"Thank you," ventured Anna, "but we could never do that. We have an old wood stove at home. It just doesn't put out much heat for the baby."

"But we'll wrap him up tightly and put him between us, and he'll be plenty warm," Donnie added.

"Okay, if you're sure," Celia gave in sluggishly. "Everyone else's gone. Why don't you come on upstairs with me?"

The teacher watched as the mother, a petite woman with thick sable-brown hair and light-brown eyes, bundled up the baby in her shawl and held him close to her breast. It tore at Celia in a way that broke her heart in two, visualizing the child, a baby with beautiful dark curls, in a home with no heat. She wanted to insist that they go home with her, but knew that was out of the question. There was no way she would intrude on their privacy, but the thought of letting them return to a house without warmth made her feel like she was abandoning them.

As she followed the couple out the school's long drive, Celia wondered whether their car, one that had obviously traveled many a mile, even had heat. Knowing her hands were tied, she tried not to think about their situation as she turned in the opposite direction from them when they got to the main highway.

Besides, I've got hot chocolate and a warm fireplace to think about, she said, heading toward her home. But she couldn't help but worry about the newborn baby as she saw their tail lights disappear in the distance.

"That does it. I can't just let them go like this," she blurted aloud, making a U-turn in the highway and hoping there were no policemen in close proximity. Celia chased Donnie down and flashed her lights at him, motioning for him to pull off the road.

He got out of his car and met her as she threw open her car's door.

"Is anything wrong, Miss Brinkley?" Donnie asked, his eyes full of the same concern that had been in hers only moments earlier when she had asked the same question.

"Yes, there certainly is," she blared. "I don't

know where my mind was a few minutes ago. There's a space heater in my office that I use to keep my feet warm under my desk. I'm not going to need it during the next couple of weeks. Let's go back to the school and get it for you to put in front of the baby's crib."

Celia had no idea what made her do it, but when they left the school for the second time, she followed at a great distance behind Donnie, determined to find the home where this family lived. There *had* to be something more she could do.

She was glad there wasn't much traffic to separate them, and that Donnie didn't take many turns while driving down the winding country backroads. As they passed several miles of farmland, Celia wondered what this place would look like in the daylight. It seemed like the kind of acreage investors were snatching up for prime ritzy developments, much like the ones where many of her students lived.

When the follower saw the brake lights come on ahead of her, and the car make a right turn before coming to a halt, Celia slowed down so the couple wouldn't notice her vehicle as she drove past the house. In the complete darkness that surrounded this place, far removed from the lights of the small town of Tillman, she couldn't tell anything about it. She went down the road a little farther looking for a driveway in which she could turn around, but it seemed there was nothing past the opening where the custodian had turned.

That's it! There's no way I'm going to leave that couple out here in the wilderness with no heat, and apparently no close neighbors. I'll bet they don't even have a telephone in case of an emergency.

Celia wheeled onto the narrow dirt driveway she had seen Donnie enter before he stopped. She had no idea what she was going to say or do when she got there, but her desperation told her she had to do something. Praying for the right words to come to her, she knocked on the door.

Donnie opened the door, obviously shocked to see anyone, much less the school's music teacher, at this time of evening.

"I'm sorry. I didn't mean to bother, but I thought maybe you could use this," Celia offered, taking her cell phone from her purse. "I didn't even think to ask whether you have a telephone here."

Anna came around the door, peeking to see what stranger had wandered up to their abode at this dark hour, way past time for callers. "Miss Brinkley?" she whispered, full of surprise.

"Yes, I brought a little something for you," the music teacher offered, trying to stumble her way through a believable excuse.

Celia retreated to her car and started digging through the packages until she found what she wanted, then grabbed the baskets and bags of delectable goodies from the front seat.

"Anna, I know you must have a million things to do with the baby, and so you won't have to wash too many dishes, I thought maybe you could use these paper products. I live all alone, so I don't have a whole lot of use for them. And there's no way I'll ever be able to eat all this food. Please take some of it so that you don't have to spend your holiday cooking. At least you'll have some wonderful breads and treats."

The couple looked at each other questioningly, but invited Celia to bring the gifts inside. Anna watched as the unexpected visitor laid out several items on a wooden table that resembled little more than a piece of plywood nailed onto two sawhorses.

"Miss Brinkley," she said, glancing at Donnie, "we couldn't possibly take all this stuff."

"Of course you can. I insist. You'll be doing me a favor. I won't have to feel bad when it goes to waste because I couldn't eat it fast enough."

"The ham was gracious plenty, Miss Brinkley," Donnie interjected.

"Man cannot live by ham alone. Here, have some of these baked goods and desserts to go with it." Celia loaded half the table with what looked like more food than she saw in the open cabinets.

In the short span of time she was in the house,

she took in every detail, feeling worse by the minute for leaving this couple, much less a newborn infant, in such a poor living condition. It seemed impossible that this man, who took care of some of the richest kids in the county by day, came to call this place home by night.

Celia noticed that there was only an old wood stove in the kitchen, realizing the same one they used for warmth was also their means for cooking their meals. The large open dining and sitting area had a sofa and a chair, and a small table that housed an old battery-operated radio like the one her grandparents had years ago. She could see there were two bedrooms in the front of the house, and she could hear the sucking, smacking sound of the baby in the one where she saw the candle's glow.

Still bothered by the scene in front of her, Celia could not shake the urge to wrap the baby up and take him to her home, to the comfort of her gas logs and soft, recessed lighting. But inwardly, she sensed there was something here that was not at her home. As she watched the mother go get the child and hold him to her breast, the discovery of an unseen, yet powerful, emotion struck her. It was the warmth and the love that only a mother could pass to a newborn infant. And it was so obvious that it was clearly visible even to a single woman who had never experienced that feeling.

Wrong, Celia. You shared this same feeling once with

your own mother. No matter that you don't remember it, it was there – unseen, yet unmistakably present, then, just as much as it is now.

Before the next words left her lips, Celia was aware of the response she would get, but she couldn't leave without again making the offer. "Donnie, I have plenty of room in my home where you and Anna would be most welcome to come and stay and bring the baby."

"Thank you, Miss Brinkley, but we have everything we need right here," the contented father answered, his wife nodding in agreement.

Celia was positive that they truly *did* have everything they needed, but she also knew how fierce the cold night temperatures could be for the tiny child. She wasn't going to force herself, or her home, on this couple, but the guest was certain that she would somehow find a way to provide a more comfortable habitat for this family.

The music teacher looked at them one last time, walking over to the mother and laying her hand on the baby's back, which was hardly bigger than her palm. "Will you please let me know if there is *anything* I can do for you?"

"We're fine," uttered Anna, smiling simply to show appreciation for the visitor's concern. "Really we are." Then the mother disappeared into one of the two front rooms with the baby.

Celia nodded her head, knowing that part of their determination came from a long heritage of pride in working for what they owned, and not accepting charity. But the bottom line was that here was a need, and the music teacher's job was to figure out how she could do something about it without offending this couple or damaging their pride.

Donnie caught her attention as he moved closer from behind. "Miss Brinkley, I hope you won't think bad of me for bringing Anna and Bobby to the school tonight and hiding them away like I did. I'm truly sorry. I hope we haven't ruined your evening."

The teacher felt a tug at her heart as she observed a look of shame, identical to the one she had seen on Donnie's face when she opened the boiler room door at the school. In her way of thinking, this man should feel neither shame nor sorrow at trying to keep his family, and especially a newborn infant, warm on a winter's night.

"Absolutely not," replied Celia. "I only wish you had all come into the auditorium and seen the program, and been more comfortable."

"Oh, we could have never done that!" he stated. "We didn't have any clothes suitable to wear to the concert."

Celia stared into Donnie's eyes, trying to read him. His choice of words made her realize that there was much more to both this man and woman than she was seeing from this poor, shabby rundown excuse for a house.

"May I see Bobby again before I go?" the visitor asked, not wanting to leave the unexplained aura of warmth she felt in this environment.

Anna, who had come back into the sitting room, led the visitor into the bedroom where Celia saw a striking antique cradle placed in front of the window. It looked totally out of place for everything else she had observed in the cabin.

"Donnie, Anna, this cradle is absolutely beautiful! Is it a family heirloom?"

"Yes," Donnie answered, bursting with pride that this object, which held great value to him, had been noticed. "I was rocked in that cradle in this same bedroom, as was my father, as were all my aunts and uncles, and brothers and sisters. The cradle was originally used for my grandfather. I uncovered it a few weeks ago out in the barn and helped Anna get it cleaned up before the baby came."

"The mattress was shot, but we've laid an old quilt that Donnie's grandmother made in the bottom of the cradle, and that works just fine," Anna added, noticeably proud of another heirloom.

Noting the look of impression on the music teacher's face, Donnie continued to share the background of his family heritage with her, hoping she might understand why they had to stay here with Bobby. "My great-grandfather built this house for my great-grand-mother when they were married. This cradle is the only thing that came from his family, and it was a great source of self-worth for him to have his offspring rocked in it. He always said it was like owning and sharing a small bit of history."

Celia began to wonder what other treasures were buried somewhere in this house, having been moved back and forth to the barn from one generation to an-other. Perhaps she could help Anna and Donnie go through the barn during Christmas vacation, and see what other useful items they could find. She made a note to come up with some brainstorm to make that idea a reality, without seeming too presumptuous.

In front of the cradle sat a small, but very de-tailed, crèche set in the window. The candle behind it gave the appearance of the star shining on the place where the baby Jesus lay. Celia thought how appropri-ate that nativity scene was. Her mind was rampant with ways of finding just the right plan to help this couple provide a more suitable environment for Bobby, but at the same time, keeping all the wonderful, heart-warm-ing elements of their home.

For in the short time she had been in the house, Celia sensed that it was filled not only with heirlooms from each generation, but decades of love and family memories, shared by the couple that now lived here. Even in their poor state, it was clear that they had a home, a home to be proud of. A home that many families – *like the ones at the school* - had missed out on completely, in spite of their very finest of dwellings and furnishings. There was a presence, an air, an odor about the house and the surroundings, something of a sweet nature. She sensed that the smell came from the hay outside in the barn.

Celia smiled to herself. All these years in teaching her students about the sweet smelling hay, she had always wondered how it could possibly smell sweet when filled by the presence of farm animals. But as she stood in this humble abode, she had been taught more than one lesson.

The music teacher knew it was time for her to leave this couple in the privacy of their own world, no matter how badly she wished she could stay. She hugged Anna and shook Donnie's hand.

"Here's my home phone number," she said, taking a card from her purse. "Keep this handy, and if you need anything, anything at all, call me. If I'm not home, leave a message. And here's the number of the cell phone should you need to give it to anyone. I don't need the phone, and no one really calls me on it. I just have it in case of an emergency on the road."

She showed Donnie how to place a call on the phone, then quietly excused herself.

As she turned the car around and headed back toward the highway, the headlights gave her a clear view of the large front porch and the cabin's old, rusted tin roof. There was a quilt, its pattern obviously antique and hand-stitched, folded and hung across the rail of the porch. Celia wondered whether one single thing had changed since the day Donnie's great-grandfather first built the house for his new bride.

The car's lights hit through the trees of the woods beside the house to reveal a deer watching her. She noticed that it moved into the front yard and stood looking toward the front bedroom window, the one with the baby, as she turned onto the main road.

Keeping watch over their flocks by night . . .

The music teacher knew that this house, this family, and this baby were being guarded, and she sensed by some force more powerful than the animals of the wild. She made her way back through the country roads singing *Away in a Manger*, hearing the angelic voices of her first graders in her mind.

Driving toward town, and the comfort of her own home, Celia decided to let the present situation go for a few minutes while she gloried in the events and the music of the evening. She could still see the faces of the children as they sang their little hearts out, their eyes sparkling as brightly as the towering tree on the stage.

There was something about the voice of a young child that still spoke to Celia in ways that were impossible with mature voices. She had never determined whether it was the simplicity, or the clarity, or the youthfulness, but she suspected it was a combination of all three. And she loved the fact that they were still too naïve to be afraid of taking chances, of singing a cappella or doing solos, and that they trusted her to give them the right notes and bring them in on cue.

The feelings and anxieties of burn-out from earlier in the evening had subsided slightly as Celia had been forced to see what a good rapport existed between she and her students. Many of them had grown up with her, and quite a few of the younger ones had older siblings that had come through her classes.

Celia began to sense that perhaps there were still some things she could share with her students. As she reflected on this, she decided that a brief Christmas vacation was exactly what she needed to get rejuvenated so she could make it until the summer, when she was thinking of making a long drive across the country. Her plan for this year's two-month break was simply to get away and let her mind wander and her body rest, instead of filling the summer weeks with her usual variety of workshops and choral festivals.

All stretched out in her chenille robe, the music teacher flipped through several pages of her new book, but somehow the words were not drawing her into the story. As she sat back in her favorite flame-stitched wing chair, resting her head against the high back, Celia took a long, slow sip of her hot chocolate, savoring every drop of its rich hazelnut flavor.

She thought back to the candlelit cabin and its contents. It suddenly struck Celia that she had entered a home in a formal gown that probably cost more than all the furnishings of that place put together. Again, the thought she had from earlier in the day ate at her.

Exactly how much money was spent on clothes for this evening's concert? she pondered. *And just how many hungry people could we have fed with all that money?*

Then Donnie's comment about "not having clothes suitable to wear to her concert" began to gnaw at her. Her mind drew a mental picture of something that had caught her attention as she was driving away from the couple's house, but it was an image that didn't speak to her until this moment. It was the candle, or rather the *glow* of the candle, in Bobby's window.

Celia remembered seeing the glow of that candle from outside, and feeling how, even in the cold surroundings with their lack of heat, that small flame gave off a warmth that reached all the way to her car. It was not the kind of warmth that came from a heater, but a feeling of supernatural warmth.

Strangely warmed. Those words came rushing back to her as she thought about the candle, and how its glow had made such an impact on her. Celia knew the warmth she had experienced, and was still experiencing, had not come solely from the wealth of love inside the cabin. It came from the same Source as the feeling she had noticed during the singing of *Gesu Bambino*.

She lowered her head. *Lord, I know there is a reason for all that has happened to me this night. I feel lots of wonder and uncertainty drifting across my mind right now. And I know that You are the only One who holds the answers to what I am supposed to do. Thank you for this awesome feeling you have given me, and please open the eyes and ears of my soul to know what to do with it.*

The questioning teacher was saddened as she thought about Donnie. She had no idea how much he made as the school's custodian, but it bothered her that he was not able to do more than he did with his paycheck. Anna was, no doubt, a housewife – *now a mother, too* – by virtue of a long-standing family tradition.

There was something more to this scenario than

met the eye, and Celia knew she could not delve into what it was any more than Donnie would allow. She gave up her idea of reading and went to bed, sure that she would have some thoughts of help come the morning.

As she lay there, the vision of the threesome in the cabin would not leave her. Unable to sleep, Celia reached in the drawer of the nightstand and took out her Bible. As was her habit when she had trouble sleeping, she opened the book and began reading where her fingers landed.

Proverbs. Good, I love those verses. Celia was sure she would find some passage that would make her feel better about the Little's situation, and would leave her with a peace so that she could relish in the blessedness of her final Christmas concert.

She began to read the fifteenth chapter aloud. Exactly halfway through the chapter, Celia found her verses. "Better *is* a little with the fear of the Lord, than great treasure with trouble. Better *is* a dinner of herbs where love is, than a fatted calf with hatred."

The reading stopped. Celia closed the book and bowed her head, sure that this was a sign that she truly *had* been "strangely warmed" this evening. Not just from the sound of the baby and the emotion of the moment at the concert, but she had *truly* been in the presence of her Lord. In His presence so strongly, in fact, that she sensed the warmth of the fire that burned within her all the way up her spine and to the very hairs on her head.

Having grown up in a Methodist home, and remembering the expression of John Wesley from her youthful confirmation days, Celia made a point of thinking back on those words – *strangely warmed*. She struggled to recall the exact description of his spiritual conversion on the blest occasion when he first felt those words.

All she could remember at the present was the fact that Wesley was prone to open his Bible and read whatever passage lay before him. That fact had tended to comfort Celia in her own Bible reading, reasoning that if it was good enough for the founder of Methodism, it was good enough for her. It had served as a bond of kinship for her in her faith. And now, as she struggled to recall the event of being "strangely warmed," she suspected there was a cause for her feeling that kinship.

She definitely had a topic of discussion she intended to pursue the next time she spoke to her minister. In fact, Celia decided she'd stay in her pew on the next Sunday, Christmas Sunday, after everyone else had left, to make sure she caught the pastor's undivided attention. By the time she went home, she intended to know all the similarities of her experience with those of the denomination's founder.

Celia put the Bible back in its place of rest, thankful for the endless messages she got from that Holy Book. Messages of grace, love, joy, forgiveness – whatever it was she needed at any given moment – that appeared at her fingertips every time she opened that drawer and began randomly reading.

She closed her eyes and remembered the young girl's simple question in song, "What can I give him?"

CHAPTER 4

While she chugged her morning coffee and walked out to get the newspaper, Celia noted the headline asking people to add extra money to their power and gas payments to help the less fortunate during the cold winter months. It immediately caught her attention as she scanned through the article that ended with a serious warning about senior citizens and infants.

Wondering how Anna and Bobby were going to stay warm during the day, she got her idea that she had prayed for the evening before. She glanced at the clock on the stove, hoping it was not too early to call. *Get a grip, Celia. This is a farmhouse we're talking about, and with a new baby at that. They've probably been up for hours.*

She couldn't help but wonder if Donnie would even answer the cell phone. In her hurry to think of an excuse for barging in last night, she failed to mention that her phone did not ring, but played a Bach toccata instead. Celia breathed a sigh of relief when she heard a male voice on the other end.

"Good morning, Donnie. I have a huge favor to ask of you."

"Miss Brinkley?"

"Yes, sorry, I forgot to identify myself," she responded, silently questioning who else would have called this family on her cell phone. "Do you think that Anna might come to school with you today and bring the baby? I'd like to have them sit in my classroom and let the students sing carols to Bobby. It would add such a creative dimension if we could use the manger and the Mary costume from last night's concert. That way, we can also make sure they stay warm during the day."

"I'm not sure, but I'll ask. Are you sure Dr. Lacey won't mind?" he asked, hesitantly.

"He's not going to say anything. You know they give me fairly free reign in coming up with hands-on examples for the music classes. And after the success of last night's concert, I seriously doubt anyone would dare say a word, even if there was a problem."

The teacher could hear voices in the background as Donnie talked to Anna about her request.

"Anna says that would be fun, if you're sure about it," came the answer.

"Oh, I'm positive. Just bring her straight to my classroom when you get to school. She can use my office to feed and change the baby, or if she needs a place to rest for a while. I have a nice comfy sofa in there."

Celia hung up, proud of her instantaneous creativity. *Too bad I can't bottle this stuff up*, she chuckled. *I could make a mint*, the teacher thought, remembering her many friends who had asked where she came up with all her ingenious ideas.

❄ ❄ ❄

Just as Celia suspected, her students loved having Anna and the baby in their classroom. Even the boys joined the girls in oohing and aahing over the baby, while he cooed back at them. They touched Bobby's tiny fingers as he held his flailing hands in the air, waving them in all directions as if he were conducting their singing of the carols.

Watching the effect this had on the children, Celia got another idea. She grabbed the phone and dialed the extension of the office assistant. "Martha, this is Celia. Is Dr. Lacey in his office?" She had skipped the formality of surnames, but everyone considered this secretary part of the family, so they all called her by her first name.

"Let me check." The office assistant was back on the line after only a few seconds. "He's on the phone, but he should be off in a couple of minutes."

"Good. Can you come down here and watch my class for a minute? I need to speak with him right away."

"I hope there's no problem," Martha replied, a hint of concern in her voice.

"Oh, no, nothing like that," Celia assured her. "It's just that I have something I want him to see in my classroom."

That was a usual request, for the music teacher was known to have something extraordinary going on with one of her groups at any given time. For that reason, it was a surefire bet that any visitors to the school, announced or otherwise, were generally herded straight to her classroom.

Martha chuckled to herself, as she made her way to the music room, thinking about when she escorted members of the accreditation committee down this hall last year, only to find Celia dressed in a black flapper dress, complete with a twenties' headband donning a huge plumed feather. Their notorious teacher was in the middle of doing the Charleston and twirling long strands of pearl beads around when the group walked into the classroom. Their wide-eyed gazes, indicating this was not their usual welcome, still stuck in the mind of the office assistant. But the committee members took a bypass to that room every day they were at the academy, noting Celia's unusual, yet most effective, teaching methods.

The office assistant walked into the classroom to find all the students quietly mesmerized by the baby in the manger. *Quite a difference from the flapper routine,* she smuggly smiled, still thinking of her memory from a second ago. She looked at Celia, questioningly, but obviously impressed.

"Martha, this is Anna Little, Donnie's wife, and their newborn son, Bobby. Anna, this is Martha Edwards, our office assistant."

"*Our* Donnie?" the assistant asked.

"One and the same," Celia nodded, glad to hear the ownership taken by Martha. "Last night, in talking to Donnie after the concert, I found out they had a new baby, so I thought this would be the perfect way to end my classes before the holiday."

The assistant shook her head as she smiled at the children, then down at the baby. Turning to Celia, she said, "I just love coming to your room. You always have the most unique lesson plans for your students."

"Yes, it's a sort of challenge for me. I think music is merely a tool to teach them all kinds of valuable lessons, most of which have to do with the world around them and their perspective of it."

Martha shook her head in amazement once again before telling all the boys and girls what a wonderful job they had done the evening before. "I'd love to have my desk in Miss Brinkley's office," she commented to the students, "just so I could watch all the cool things you do every day."

"This baby is the *coolest*!" one of the little girls squealed, like she had her very own doll to play with in class. Both the music teacher and the assistant grinned at the child's response.

Celia excused herself and hurriedly walked to the headmaster's office before he had time to get called away to some other duty. Seeing Dr. Lacey at his desk, she tapped lightly on his door, hoping to draw his attention away from the papers that lay in front of him.

"Well, if it isn't our very own star!" he acknowledged, looking over his glasses while getting up and extending his hand.

The music teacher lowered her head and explained, "I'm only an instrument. The children are the real stars. I couldn't do my job without them, and our concerts wouldn't be so spectacular without all their hard work."

"That's true," he agreed, motioning his hand for her to sit, "but they can only accomplish what you encourage them to do. Celia, you must take more ownership in your work."

What the headmaster didn't understand was that Celia saw her work as an extension of the blessings granted by the One whom she thanked each morning and evening. However, she chose not to have that discussion with him at the moment.

Not taking the time to sit, she proceeded directly to her purpose for the unexpected visit. "Could you come down to my classroom? The children and I have a holiday surprise for you." The teacher knew she would get no objection, for the administrator took great pride in watching the students perform. Celia had appreciated that sincerity in him from the day she was hired, for she knew his interest in them went far beyond the normal job description.

Here is a man who has truly followed his calling, Celia mused as they walked down the hall in conversation. *How perfectly suited he is for his job, and how much more fitting it seems for him to be in a private facility rather than a public school.* She couldn't help but hope that when this time came next year, she would be thinking the same thing about her own self in regards to following her calling.

As they neared Celia's room, she asked Dr. Lacey

to wait for a second before entering so that she could get the students ready. When she opened the door, the children stood nestled around the manger singing in their most gentle, pure tones on *Away in a Manger*.

The headmaster was as touched by this outpouring of love from the children as Martha had been. Celia went on to make the introduction, and tell him how the baby and mother had come to be a part of her latest wild-haired idea for a teaching session.

Pleased that he was not the least bit upset, the music teacher knew she had the go-ahead to proceed with the rest of her ploy, a plan that had evolved in her head since the arrival of the mother and baby that morning.

After Dr. Lacey told the students what a terrific job they had done the evening before, and how well they had represented the school, Celia asked to speak to him for a minute. He followed her to her office in the back of the classroom and sat down as she closed the door behind them.

"Dr. Lacey, is the school really as interested in being involved in an outreach program as some of the staff has indicated at the faculty meetings?"

"Yes, there is a committee looking into different ideas now. We hope to begin with something by the end of January, kicking it off when we come back after the holidays."

"Hmmm . . ."

The headmaster could see the gears turning in her head as her eyes glanced toward the window and her lips squeezed together in a distorted shape.

"Okay, Celia, spit it out. I know you have something cooking in that creative mind of yours."

"Well, first off, you know what they say about committees, so that could stand in the way of my idea."

"No, I don't know what they say about committees, so why don't you tell me, and we'll go from there," Dr. Lacey encouraged.

Celia took a small wooden plaque from her desk drawer and handed it to her boss. It read: *Camel – a racehorse designed by a committee.*

Dr. Lacey broke into laughter. As much as he hated to agree with the musician's non-conformist ideas, he did have to admit that this statement held true more often than not.

"I have a plan that could provide us with a most unique outreach project, one that would give all the students a hands-on experience, and that the entire community could get involved in." Celia plowed forward. "*And* we can start immediately."

"It's obvious you have already worked this out in great detail. Let me hear your idea, and if it's feasible, I'll see what I can do about the committee," the headmaster compromised.

"I'll go you one better than that," offered Celia. "Why don't you call the members down here right now and I'll explain the whole plan to you at one time? It won't take but a few minutes."

She could see the look of uncertainty on his face. Her mind quickly raced to come up with her next supporting statement. "Look. All the teachers have volunteers in their rooms to cover for them during the luncheon, so this should not cause a problem. Besides, it's the day before Christmas break, so how retentive do you realistically think the children are going to be at this point?"

Celia had been at the school long enough to make her mark. Although she did have some hair-brained ideas from time to time, she came up with a lot of programs that got the school much positive attention. Perhaps she really did hold the key to getting this private school, looked upon by some in the town as a junior country club, recognized as an establishment that cared about the community.

Dr. Lacey opened the door and motioned for the office assistant.

"Martha, go back to the office and buzz the teachers on the outreach committee. Ask them to come down here for a few minutes. There are enough volunteers setting up for parties to watch their classes that long."

"Yes, sir," she energetically responded, wondering what was going on, but not about to ask, as she headed off to the office to carry out her assignment. *Whatever this is, it must be pretty important, and I'll bet it involves that mother and baby,* she thought, walking down the hall, *and Celia Brinkley!* she chuckled to herself, anxious to see what the eccentric music teacher was up to this time.

❄ ❄ ❄

When all the committee members had assembled in Celia's room, she instructed the students to sing a few carols around the manger. The teachers looked on the scene, which was an equally beautiful and heartwarming sight, and commented on how realistic this made the meaning of the carols for the children.

Great, just what I wanted, Celia thought as she motioned them to her office.

Dr. Lacey, and the four teachers who made up the outreach committee, listened intently as the music teacher told them about what she had found the night before. As the woman in front of them proceeded to unfold her magnificent proposal, it proved to be a plan that wholeheartedly intrigued these individuals who were, as usual, amazed by Miss Brinkley's brainstorms.

Brad Simms, the phys ed teacher was the first one to speak. "I think she's got a plan."

Celia wondered whether the stereotypical jock really liked the idea, or if he was merely excited at the thought of no more committee meetings. Before she had time to come to a conclusion, Roberta Gaye, chairperson of the committee, expounded on his comment.

"I don't know about the rest of you, but I think Celia's right. This fills all our criteria for the example we've been hoping to set for the community, and it meets the need of someone within our own organization. It allows the children an opportunity to do more than just give a hand-out to someone, and it provides the entire school family and community a chance to take ownership in this project, rather than simply dole out money for yet another social concern."

Dr. Lacey could see the other heads nodding in agreement. "It looks to me as if this is settled. All in favor, say aye."

There was no question as to the outcome of the vote.

"Thanks," the headmaster noted, speaking to the committee members. He then turned to the music teacher. "Celia, you get a memo for the students drawn up immediately so they can take it home today. Of course, after I go to each classroom to tell the students about this, I doubt there's one home in this entire school family that doesn't have your project as the topic of dinnertime discussion."

That's what I like about this man, Celia thought. *He really gets involved in every single activity.*

Dr. Lacey looked at the chairperson of the committee. "Mrs. Gaye, can you write up the minutes of this meeting so we can have them on file?"

"I'll take care of that since I'm our newly elected secretary," volunteered one of the other teachers.

"Great. I'll go and begin my visit to the classrooms," Dr. Lacey finished. He turned and winked at Celia. "There are days that I absolutely *love* my job."

The teachers all glanced at each other, smirking and nodding in agreement with the headmaster. They all knew he loved his job, and as far as he was concerned, this was simply another routine duty.

"I think it's grand that this will take precedence over their school parties," one of the members commented as she walked out the door.

"Yes, this is exactly how it's supposed to feel when you do an outreach project," another added.

Celia smiled to herself. *You ain't seen nothing yet!* she beamed, knowing the impact of what was to come.

The statement that shocked Celia the most was the one she heard from the phys ed teacher as he was going out the door, "This is what Christmas is all about."

Perhaps the man has a heart and a soul after all. Maybe he's the one I need to recruit to help me with this project, the music teacher noted, as she decided to chat with him after school that afternoon.

"Mrs. Gaye, do you have a minute?" Celia called to the school's head of curriculum.

"As a matter of fact, I do. I wanted to tell you how pleased I am with your idea, anyway."

The music teacher offered a gingerly "thank you" as she bowed her head slightly. "That's what I wanted to talk to you about," Celia added in a tentative voice. "Mrs. Gaye, I know you are a believer, and I know you can relate to the Source of this brainstorm as much as I. This entire situation has moved me from the time I first heard the baby cry last night. Never in my life have I felt the Holy Spirit's presence as vibrantly as I have in the past day. It hasn't even been twenty-four hours yet, and I feel like a new person ... or at least a *different* person.

"In our denomination, there's a story about our founder being 'strangely warmed.' That's how I've felt with all of this. In fact, I've already made plans to speak to the minister after the worship service on Sunday. I know there's a connection here somewhere between my experience and that of John Wesley."

"I have no doubt there is," Mrs. Gaye offered. "I've watched you at work during your tenure here, and much of what you do is motivated by your faith, sometimes quietly and sometimes not so quietly. I'm not sure how many of the others noticed, but the glow on your face as you made your presentation to us said all we needed to know about this outreach project. I feel certain that you were simply given the role of a messenger from above."

"You know, I've always admired you." Celia said humbly. "From the moment I first met you, you've served as a mentor to me. And I've watched closely when other teachers have come to you for advice. You've not once belittled anyone on our staff, you've offered encouragement to all of us, and your role as a leader over the academic program these past few years has been an asset to the entire school family."

Celia's eyes spoke of her sincere esteem for her mentor. "Your comment today regarding this proposal meant more to me than you'll ever know. I highly respect your opinion, and to hear that approval from you convinced me that I wasn't too far out in left field with my idea."

"No, Miss Brinkley, not at all. As I said, this was not solely your idea."

"Thank you." Celia's head was not bowed this time as she said the words, her smile showing a comfort in its gleam. She glanced at her watch. "I'd better get to work if I'm going to make this thing happen."

"Don't worry, it'll happen," assured Mrs. Gaye. "And let me know what I can do to help."

"Sure thing," the music teacher added, already

reaching for the pen and paper on her desk.

Luckily, it was time for her morning break. The crafty musician quickly drafted a letter to the students and their parents outlining her plan and giving them all the specific details. She decided to leave it in its handwritten form, hoping it would have more of a personal impact. After taking it to Martha to make copies, Celia went down her list making assignments for certain students.

The first ones on her list were the six boys who had sung in the ensemble the evening before. It just so happened that each of them had a special gift at their disposal of which she intended to make use.

Next, she called her friends at the local newspaper and the radio station to make a public announcement about the school's unique outreach opportunity. Celia wished to request the community's involvement through their support, praying that Donnie and Anna didn't subscribe to the newspaper, and that their car radio didn't work.

Pleased with what she had accomplished in her forty-five minute break, she made a second list of things to do and people to call when the school day was over. Realizing she needed some help with all of the necessary contacts, Celia decided to make use of all the members on the outreach committee, glad she had finally learned to delegate after all these years of teaching.

And what a shame it had to be now, just as I was getting ready to leave this profession! she laughed. *Oh well, maybe that ability will come in handy in my next line of work,* Celia concluded, preparing her mind for another group of children and their reaction to the *real* blessed baby in her room.

Before the day was over, the determined music teacher had enlisted the willingness of nearly every person on the school's staff to help with her endeavor. Having been afraid they would be too busy with holiday preparations or travel plans, Celia was thrilled that they all wanted to participate in the school's outreach effort. Being careful not to let Anna hear, several of the teachers made a special trip by the music room to congratulate their colleague on such a brilliant and ingenuous idea.

Celia wanted to explain that this was not *her* idea, but merely a way of responding by what came as a natural reaction to her discovery. She was absolutely sure God had allowed her to find Donnie and his family in the boiler room, knowing she would follow her instincts and do something to help them in their time of need.

Her watchful eyes observed the custodian during the day, scurrying around the school while helping volunteers get ready for parties, cleaning up afterwards, and assisting teachers in getting bags of presents to their cars. She also felt sure she was merely doing what he would do for someone else, given the opportunity.

When her classes were over for the day, Celia offered to take Anna and Bobby home. She knew Donnie's chores would include closing up the school for the holidays before he could leave.

"Why don't you let me call Donnie to my room so you can tell him what's going on, and have a few minutes alone with him?" she asked Anna. "I still need to see one more teacher before I leave."

"Miss Brinkley, you've already gone to so much trouble for us. I don't want to put you out anymore."

"I insist. Besides, I'm sure he'd love a break and a chance to see his family, and that would give me just enough time to finish up here."

Anna saw there was no use trying to change the music teacher's mind, and she had to admit she was anxious to see her husband.

Celia took off for the gym, hoping to catch Brad before he got out the door. She knew that he, too, was single, and she was unsure whether he had a hot date for the evening, or would be heading straight out the door to visit his family during the break. Either way, she was going to make her pitch. After his comment earlier in the day, she was confident he would not scoff at her.

Seeing a light in the coach's office, she made her way confidently to the door.

"Celia," he called to her, looking up from his grade book. "I don't see you down here much." He paused for a brief second, then added, "In fact, I don't recall seeing you down here at all."

She felt a sigh of relief that he even knew her first name. Knowing the students were all gone, Celia felt she could return the casualness.

"Yeah, well, you know how it is. Most of us musicians are *not* the greatest athletes in the world. And you're right. Since the dedication for the school last August, this is the first time I've been back here."

"Uh-huh," Brad smirked, playfully giving her a hard time, which she saw straight through. "So what brings you down here now?"

"Ah, c'mon. You know we resource teachers are so busy around here that we can barely keep up with ourselves, much less make social calls on the other teachers," she responded, adding a quick grin, not wanting him to think she was being short.

He returned her grin. "Back to the question. So what brings you down to the *other* side of the campus this afternoon? Surely you didn't make the trek all the way out here just to wish me a Merry Christmas."

"No, I didn't," she laughed, "but while I'm out

here, that's a good idea. Merry Christmas, Brad!"

"Merry Christmas to you, too, Celia Brinkley. Now that that's out of the way, why are you *really* here?"

Celia felt they had sufficiently broken the ice between them, so she went straight to her point. "I came to see if you might be available to help me on Friday evening. Like me, you have to work with all the grade levels, so you know each of the students by name. I sure could use some help herding up all those kids before our little outreach project begins."

"So you thought I was the man for the job?" Brad asked, still full of humor.

"Yes, I guess you could put it that way," Celia answered, learning to appreciate the light-hearted personality of this person she had always considered the "dumb jock." "I wasn't sure whether you would be going home for Christmas or what," she added, realizing that she didn't have a clue as to where home was for this fellow teacher.

"I *am* going to see my family, but not until Christmas Day. I'll tell you what. Why don't we discuss this over dinner tomorrow evening?"

Brad's question caught Celia completely off guard. She had only spoken to this man in the hallway, and she knew nothing of him, except that the students apparently loved being with him, given their flattering comments. And now, that was an opinion she shared after seeing his easy going and jovial manner. The musician wasn't sure whether or not to accept the invitation, between her own shopping and all that had to be organized before Friday evening.

"It's not that I don't appreciate the offer, but I haven't even started my Christmas shopping yet. And I feel there's going to be a ton of items to take care of before Friday night. I just don't,"

"Tell ya what I'm a-gonna do fer ya, little lady." Brad cut her off in a tone that sounded like a cross between W. C. Fields, John Wayne and a ringmaster. "Just because I like ya, and I believe so much in what yer tryin' to do here, I'm a-gonna let you go shopping with me after dinner tomorrow evening. But that's only after we've taken care of all your business tomorrow, do ya hear?"

Celia was bursting in laughter as she watched the PE teacher pretend to flick ashes off the end of a cigar. She knew there was no getting out of the invitation, and at this point, she wasn't sure she even wanted to try.

"Okay, you've got yourself a deal," she nodded. "But only because you insist."

"Yes, I *do* insist, Miss Brinkley," Brad said, standing from behind his desk. I was really touched by your idea today and I've given it lots of thought since then. I'd love to help with this adventure on Friday evening."

For the first time in the three years she had known Brad Simms, Celia actually took a long, hard look at him. She had heard the numerous remarks from all the other female teachers about wishing they could feel his muscles, or about what a hunk he was. But she had honestly paid him no attention, having been more attracted to intellectual beings that appreciated the arts.

Dressed in khaki shorts, and a navy cotton sweater with a white golf shirt's collar sticking out at the neck, his tussled brown hair looked like he had spent the day out on a sailboat rather than the soccer field with his students. He was extremely tanned from all the time he had spent outdoors, a feature that was enhanced by the contrast of his grayish-colored eyes that picked up hints of blue from the sweater.

Celia found herself wondering why he wasn't already occupied for the next evening, but decided she had left Anna and Bobby long enough, and she was sure Donnie needed to get back to work.

She put out her hand. "I guess you've got yourself a date, Bradley Simms," hoping she hadn't made a poor choice of words.

"Why don't I meet you here around nine in the morning?" he asked.

"Why don't you come over to my place?" Celia suggested. "I want to make some calls about Friday before I go shopping. This project really *has* become my number one priority."

"Okay. You've got yourself a deal," Brad agreed. "We'll spend the day taking care of business, then go get a bite and do some shopping after you've finished all you want to get done. The stores are open late this close to the holidays."

The music teacher smiled, touched by this man's genuine interest in her effort to help a needy family. She started to walk away, then stuck her head back in the door. "I live on,"

"I know. Dr. Lacey pointed out your house while giving me the grand tour of the town when I first moved here."

Celia nodded and headed back toward her classroom, glad that she had another willing body to help with her project. *And what a bod it is,* she joked with herself, thinking about what all the other teachers would say if they knew what had just happened. She thanked God that in addition to recruiting a helper, she had also experienced a meeting of the Spirit with another person.

The teacher realized that not only had she made another friend, and seen that he was something other than what he seemed, but she had learned a lesson about herself. In thinking of the students and their families, she had no idea of what was in their hearts.

Have I become so hard-hearted and judgmental over

these years of watching them that I've cultivated a biased attitude, based on a few of them?

For the first time, Celia figured out that she had gotten so caught up in helping Donnie and Anna, in order to give Bobby a better future, that she had placed the cart before the horse. She definitely felt a calling as a spiritual believer to reach out to them, to help them. And she felt the calling as a teacher to give her students a lesson far more meaningful than any song or background of a famous composer.

Her soul asked her mind why she had those callings. *Where did they come from?* she heard from somewhere inside herself. Although she knew the answer to the question, her mind was forcing her to focus on a point that she had missed.

Celia stopped dead in her tracks. The experienced teacher knew what had suddenly come over her. It was the same thing that happened every time she tried to offer the students a special lesson. She was the one who inevitably learned the greatest lesson.

With that thought, her feet pivoted as she turned and headed back toward the gym and Brad's office. She rushed into his room, grabbed the phone, and buzzed the front office.

"Martha," she said as soon as she heard the familiar voice, "would you please make an announcement for all teachers who are still on campus to meet for a couple of minutes in the gym?"

The office assistant heard an edge of urgency in Celia's voice. For the second time in the past few hours, she wondered what was going on with the music teacher. But given what had transpired during the course of the day, Martha assumed it was an announcement regarding Friday evening, so she granted the musician's request with no questions.

When Celia hung up the phone, Brad reached over to her, took her arm, and turned her gently so that she faced him. "Are you alright, Celia?" he asked, a look of deep concern and tenderness in his eyes. "You look as if you've seen a ghost."

She sighed reflectively, shaking her head while looking at the floor. "I have, of sorts," Celia answered, knowing her candid remark may have just cost her a dinner date, but more importantly, a comrade for her mission.

Brad didn't say any more, seeing that she was deep in thought, and figuring he would hear everything he needed to know when all the other teachers arrived. He looked carefully at the music teacher, seeing a transformation in her from a few minutes earlier. But deciding it didn't look like one of fear, he relaxed with a slight sense of relief.

Once the handful of teachers had assembled in the gym, all sharing where they were going, how they were going to spend the holidays, and comparing how much they still had to do to make Christmas happen, Celia felt more sure of the need for her meeting.

It had continually intrigued the music teacher, with a growing fascination each year, to hear people talk about what they had to do to make Christmas happen. That blessed day was going to come whether they were ready for it or not. Just like any baby, it came in its due time and didn't wait for anyone's permission. Not only that, she felt strongly that its arrival would have much more of an effect if people didn't spend so much time "making" it happen, but simply "letting" it happen.

Celia wanted to make that point, but decided against it, for the reason of her meeting would take care of that in unspoken words. *The way all things should be communicated,* she mused, remembering the quote of Saint Francis challenging people to "preach the gospel everyday. Use words when necessary."

Speaking in a different tone from what she had with the outreach committee, Celia's words began.

Brad wondered whether she had come to her senses and realized what a monumental task she had set up for herself. But as he listened, he heard a far more relaxed slant in her voice. *No,* he thought, *she has this completely under control.*

"Thank you for taking the time to come down

here. Donnie and Anna are in my room with Bobby, so I didn't feel I could ask you to come there. It dawned on me a few minutes ago that I had been so busy thinking of what we needed to do for this couple, and their newborn, that I had approached it as if it were one of my staged productions. Because of that, I had thrown my creative juices into overdrive. But this is not a staged event. It is a mission. In order for it to accomplish what we really want it to, it has to be led by prayer, and it has to be of the Father of the child – the *real* Father of Bobby. Would you all please join me in a brief prayer?"

Dear Lord, you are the only One who can enable us to accomplish what we hope to do for this family, for Donnie and Anna and Bobby, in this short time span. Help us to realize the reason for this mission, just as we remind ourselves of the reason for this season. And in so doing, let us be mindful that we are seeking help for these people in need, offering an opportunity for others to bring a gift and follow in Christ's example of love, and putting all desires for our own recognition, and the recognition of Tillman Academy aside. Guide us and direct us in every effort we make toward this mission of outreach, and touch the people's hearts whom we contact so that they will also be willing to reach out to this family, and to others around them, not only during this holiday season, but throughout each and every day.

After the "amen", and she saw heads begin to slowly rise, the music teacher challenged each of the other teachers and Martha, whose curiosity had gotten the best of her, to pray individually for Friday evening, and for she, and others who would be contacting prospective donors, to look for leadership from the right Source.

The teachers left, each hugging Celia and expressing a wish for the outcome of the mission project, while promising to meet her challenge. She realized how fortunate she was to teach in a private school that housed believers and encouraged programs and events to nurture the students in their own beliefs. Had she been in many situations, the musician was conscious that her "prayer meeting" would have never happened.

Mrs. Gaye took Celia's hand and squeezed it. "Miss Brinkley, God is with you, and will *continue* to be with you, in this endeavor."

The look in her eyes, and the tone of her voice, told the music teacher that this wise mentor sensed what was going on inside her. Having been in this position for as many years as the seasoned educator had, this was surely not the first time she had encountered the symptoms of burn-out. Celia didn't try to make a vocal response, but returned the look of care and compassion expressed in Mrs. Gaye's face, as she squeezed back on the hand that held hers.

Once the teachers were all out of earshot, the musician turned to Brad. "I hope this doesn't change your mind about tomorrow. But if it does, I understand. You are welcome to back out of your offer."

He looked at Celia with eyes that spoke of a deep longing, one that she did not understand. "No, it doesn't change a thing." Brad paused, as he looked past the music teacher and fixed his eyes on the wall beyond her. "Well, at least it doesn't change our plans for shopping and a meal. But I have a story I want to tell you tomorrow evening over dinner. I think you'll really appreciate it."

Celia smiled. "Brad, I'm looking forward to tomorrow."

"Me, too . . . for several reasons," he responded, full of thought.

CHAPTER 5

Celia dropped Anna off, with instructions that she would be bringing vegetables to go with the ham for dinner, and that she had something special she wanted to share with the couple.

"Miss Brinkley, you really don't have to make such a fuss over us. We're all fine and I can fix dinner."

"I know that," Celia answered, staring into the cradle, "but it's so much fun to do things for the parents of this little guy. It makes me feel good just by being around you. Besides, thanks to me, you and your little fellow have had a long day. The least I can do is bring dinner so that you can rest and spend some time alone with your child."

While Anna went back to the car for her bag, it gave the teacher a chance to look around a little more closely, making mental notes of repairs to be made. She eyed the small cabin, sparsely furnished. What pieces there were had obviously been well used through several generations. The cracks and holes around the outside walls indicated that this place had housed as many creatures on the inside as it had on the outside. Celia allowed that thought to vanish, given her phobia of rodents and the realization that there were probably several pairs of tiny eyes observing her from hidden places as she stood there.

She drove back to town, hoping that the department store in the local mall, tiny as it might be, had the gift she was looking for. Celia had decided there was something Bobby needed to go with the crèche in the windowsill, and she was exactly the person to give it to him. If her brainstorm worked "according to Hoyle," as the expression went, this little guy was going to be the recipient of many gifts over the next few days, and she wanted him, *and his parents*, to get used to the showering of love they were about to receive.

The teacher hoped that her plan would not totally overwhelm the couple, nor embarrass them, and she especially hoped it wouldn't offend them. But she prayed that the Giver of all gifts would take care of that part of the plan for her. Regardless, she had to move forward, for it was like her conscience would not let go of this project now. She thought about all the times she had been upset at people bringing her gifts, *like last night*, but later realized that it must have given the bearers a good feeling. *Like now, for instance*, for she was so excited, Celia felt she could explode.

By the time she left the mall, Bobby's wrapped gift in hand, the wheels inside her mind were busily turning. Her brainstorm - *No! God's planting of a seed*, her mind corrected her - was forming into a massive undertaking, but Celia was sure she could handle it.

This is going to be my *Christmas . . . for many reasons.* She smiled as she remembered hearing those last three words a little earlier, and made a vow that it mattered not how much time she poured into this effort.

She decided to go home, change clothes, and take a few minutes to make some necessary phone calls to get the ball rolling in her search for prospective donors.

Celia was all smiles as she left to go back to the Little's cabin. As ecstatic as she was that her percentage rate of acceptance offers was batting a thousand, she was not really surprised. It was obvious to her that, as with her music, she felt she was being used as an instrument for a greater plan. There was no doubt in her mind about the origin of her idea, or Who was in charge of all the events beginning to surround it.

What if they turn me down? she questioned for the first time as she drove in the driveway of the couple. *They may not want to have a public spectacle made of their little bundle of joy.* Celia decided not to let her mind run away with negative thoughts. She would know of the Little's decision before the evening was over. Then, *if necessary*, she could come up with a Plan B.

Besides, if I am being used for a greater plan, there's no way this can fail, she convinced herself, her confidence mounting.

The young couple was getting used to Celia showing up at their front door, bearing gifts. This evening was no different. Not only did she prepare the dinner meal, but she also brought a present for the baby, and one for the house.

Anna beamed with delight when the music teacher hung the wreath from her classroom on the front door of the cabin. Nestled between perfectly shaped fir trees on either side of the house, and the red cardinal sitting in the berry-laden holly tree in the front yard, the house took on a natural 'Christmasy' feel.

Then the proud mother unwrapped Bobby's gift to reveal a musical mobile with animals that would circle around the top of her son's cradle while lulling him to sleep. Donnie immediately put the pieces of the mobile together and hung it from the top of the cradle. He wound the key so that the animals began to move to the music. The parents anxiously watched as Bobby's ears searched for the source of the music and his young eyes strained to make out the animals as they passed over his head.

Celia loved the enthusiasm that was shown in the acceptance of her gifts. *Maybe Friday night won't be so bad, after all.* She breathed a sigh of relief, feeling less apprehensive about the couple's reaction to the school's project.

The teacher loved rocking Bobby while Donnie and Anna ate the candlelight dinner she had prepared for them. She was not used to infants, but the art of holding the baby and singing soft lullabies came naturally to her. Celia laughed inwardly, figuring women must come equipped with that innate ability. Then as she smiled down at the cooing child, she regretfully realized that she was wrong in her assumption.

What had she first thought when she heard the baby? What had she feared she would find? *No*, she corrected herself, *there are far too many women who don't want their babies, or that have no clue as to what a precious gift their offspring are.*

Celia began to ponder on the act of creation, and what a blessed privilege it was. She wouldn't have minded having children, but she had never found the partner she felt was meant for her. Thus, she had become content to be a mother to all her students. And now, the teacher was quite comfortable with her single lifestyle.

Her mind turned to her friend, one of her co-workers at the school, who so desperately wanted a child, and had tried every possible option over the past few years, hoping to conceive. It saddened Celia greatly to think of how many desperate couples suffered from infertility, and why there were so many unwanted babies in the world. Her heart ached as she held Bobby, and prayed for unwanted babies, and then for want-to-be parents throughout the world.

As she glanced over at the couple exchanging looks of deep devotion and appreciation back and forth to each other, she sensed an even stronger ambience about this place that was absent from her home. Even though this was not the height of comfort that she felt the baby needed, this was home to Donnie and Anna. This had served as home to Donnie's ancestors for several decades, so it must have been a real slap in his face when she suggested that he come and bring his family to her place – *heat or no heat.*

But then, surely he has to know this baby needs the advantages of heat, electricity, and telephone service. Her eyes fixed on the couple for a moment. *Or perhaps not. Donnie and Anna look most content without those commodities,* Celia told herself, finding that hard to imagine in a modern lifestyle, even for a rural cabin buried back in the country.

She revisited the evening before when she had stopped Donnie on the road and suggested they go back to the school and get the space heater. He didn't mention a word about having no electricity.

Was that to get me off his back? Or was he that embarrassed about their living conditions?

Celia paused, trying to put herself in his place, but with no success. The teacher had no idea how they had gotten to this point, so there was no way she could try to imitate his situation in her mind. But what she did know was that he surely didn't expect her to pull up in his driveway last night and knock on the door, close to the midnight hour, thereby catching them unaware.

Suddenly, she was not sure her brainstorm was such a fine idea. What if Donnie saw it in a totally different light from what she meant it? Celia sat rocking Bobby, looking into his face, as if *there* she could find her answer to the present dilemma. Then she thought about her own question. *In a totally different light. Totally light. Light.*

That's it! she concluded. I mean this as a true gift of love and appreciation for this couple and their newborn son. The time I have spent with them has made me even more aware of what a perfect place this is for them. What I want to do comes from the heart, with only the best of intentions. I'll depend on the Light, the same Light that came into the world with that baby long ago, to use my words to give the right meaning to Donnie and Anna. And I'll also depend on that Light to touch their hearts, and let them know this is not a hand-out, but a gift of sacred love.

Her mind was made up. She would wait until they had finished the cherry cheesecake she had made for dessert, and then she would present the plan. *Or part of it.* The rest they would learn about *after* it happened, and they had seen for themselves, *firsthand*, that it had all happened because of the heart-warming effect that Bobby's story had on this small community.

Celia crooned lullabies to the baby as his parents finished their candlelight feast. *Hush, little baby, don't say a word*, she sang, *Mama's going to buy you a mockingbird*, and thought about all the gifts that would be showered on Bobby and this family before too much longer.

When the couple joined her in the sitting area,

Celia asked them if they would be available in a couple of evenings for a little gathering she had planned at the school. "It's actually for the community," she explained. "I had thought what a tremendous gift our students could give the surrounding area by doing a live nativity. And you and Bobby would be perfect for our Holy Family."

Donnie and Anna looked at each other, touched by the offer, as they listened to their guest offer encouragement.

"It's supposed to get close to the freezing mark, but we'll make sure the baby stays warm, as well as the two of you. We have robes at the school that our Mary and Joseph characters used for the Christmas concert. You could put them on over your clothes. And one of the fathers has offered the use of a free-standing heater to put beside the three of you."

She looked at their faces, hoping to see any hint of acceptance.

The husband stared at his wife, not wanting to make a decision without her input. "Well, we *don't* have any plans for Friday evening," Donnie offered sheepishly, inviting his spouse's opinion.

Anna looked at him, trying to weigh his unspoken expression before making any comments. "The children were so adorable as they sang to Bobby at school today. They really seemed to love the baby."

"Oh, we *all* love the baby. He made not only the day, but the entire season have meaning for everyone at the school," Celia reaffirmed.

"Well then, I guess it's settled," answered Donnie. "What time shall we be there?"

Celia breathed a sigh of relief, knowing that her plan - *wrong, His plan!* - was going to work. "Why don't you come about six? We're advertising the nativity to be from 6:30 until 8:30 so that people have time to get home from work and grab a bite before they come. And it will be over in time for the children to get home and go to bed before it's too late."

"We'd love to do this," added Anna. "What a story to tell little Bobby when he gets older. I hope someone will take pictures for us to show him."

"I'll make sure of that," assured the teacher. "In fact, there will probably be a vast assortment of cameras and videos on hand for the event. There's even talk of reporters being there from the newspaper and the local TV station."

"Wow," exclaimed Anna, "our Bobby may be on television before he's a month old."

"Oh, I'm sure he probably will," Celia nodded, knowing that the star of the show was certain to be shown on the news. She secretly hoped that the couple in front of her would not be angry at the rest of the story. Then it struck the teacher that there was no television in the place for the two of them to watch, even with electricity. Her mental list grew to include having a television delivered to the home during the live nativity, at the same time the utilities would all be hooked up.

She sat, watching Anna feed the baby, with Donnie standing over the mother's shoulder and holding onto Bobby's tiny finger. It seemed strange to her that both of these adults apparently were fairly well educated. They could carry on a decent conversation, void of most of the slangs and contractions she heard from many people in the remote areas of this county. A part of her continued to wonder how they came to be in this dire hardship.

As if he were reading her mind, Donnie came and sat beside her on the old threadbare sofa. "Miss Brinkley, I have something I'd like to tell you."

"Call me Celia, please. We're not in front of the students, so there's no code of professional ethics here."

He nodded. "I feel I must make an explanation to you."

The teacher needed no explanations and wondered why he felt that was necessary, but Celia gathered it was more for his benefit than hers, so she sat back and listened.

"As I mentioned last night, my great-grandfather built this cabin as a wedding gift for my great-grandmother. They raised eight children here, and had five others either stillborn, or that didn't make it past two years. And all their grandkids practically grew up here, because my aunts and uncles lived on the surrounding land and everybody farmed together."

The same tone of pride that had been present in Donnie's voice the evening before, when he talked about the cradle, was now evident in this story. "My grandfather inherited this place, and all of us grandchildren spent our entire summers here, the girls helping Grandmaw and the boys helping Grandpaw, so it's like we grew up here, too.

"In its day, it was a fine farmhouse to be looked up to by the neighbors. But my grandfather grew to be a ripe old age, as did my grandmother, and they got to the point they could no longer care for the house. It got rundown over the years, for they refused to let their children come in and do their work. That was just the way of my folks. After my Grandmaw died, the house sat vacant for quite a few years while the family decided what to do with the property, causing it to get more rundown."

Donnie's words seemed to be picking up steam as he outlined the history of his family and this home down through the generations.

"My father had wanted this place since he was a child. So he worked out a fair deal with his brothers and sisters and took out a mortgage on it. Although the house wasn't worth a lot, all the land cost a pretty penny."

The teacher glanced over to the wall. Family pictures displayed the characters she was hearing about, allowing her to feel a slight closeness to them.

"His intention was to fix the place up, remodel everything, and make it the fine home place it had been when it was first built. He and Mom got right to work, anxious to make his plans on draft paper a reality. I had just gone off to college, so I wasn't home to help.

"Anyway, right after he got the place, and he and my mom sold all their belongings and moved here, my mom took sick. They didn't think too much about it at first, but as time passed and she didn't get any better, my father took her to the doctor. It seemed she had developed some rare blood disease that took a lot of care for several years."

Celia caught the words "off to college." She had been right in her assumption that this guy had some education. Her ears stayed perked, lest she miss any details of his story.

"I wanted to come home after my first semester to help out," Donnie's voice trailed on, "but Dad insisted that his son *would* go to college. For his sake, I continued the second semester. When I came home for the summer, it became obvious how quickly Mom had gone downhill, and I begged my dad to let me stay here and do my part to help, not only with this place, but her. He still would hear none of that."

A deep sigh preceded his next words. "She took such constant attention, within months, that he couldn't get far away from her at any one time to do anything." His speech slowed, as the intensity of the story grew. "I think he began to see that his dream of fixing up the cabin, at least for the time being, wasn't going to materialize. But he loved my mother dearly, and their time together was worth more than anything he could have done on the house."

As Celia listened to Donnie's story, seeing that he needed to tell it, to get it out of his system, she noticed that his face didn't carry a pained expression, but rather a matter-of-factly fixed gaze. It proved to her that his mission of staying here and making this a respectable home was as much for his father as it was for himself.

"However, the medical bills began to drain their funds that had been planned for home improvement expenses. My dad had worked in the local mill, so my folks weren't what you'd call rich, but Dad had worked hard, and saved all he could, so they felt comfortable with their retirement. He had planned to work some, enough to pay the mortgage each month, figuring he'd have enough other income from his pension and social security. But that income began to look pretty meager in comparison to all the medicine, and doctor and hospital bills. Their insurance wasn't the best in the world, so it left a lot of expenses uncovered. The insurance company found all kinds of loopholes for not paying, and Dad didn't have the money or energy to fight them, 'cause he was too busy taking care of Mom."

Celia hurt so badly for this family that she felt herself wanting to cry, but she didn't dare, at least in Donnie's presence.

"But at the same time, he refused to put a price tag on my mother's quality of life, and as long as he was physically able, he tried to ensure that she had something worth living for, determined never to let her know how bad the financial affair was."

Donnie's head lowered, not in embarrassment, but from feeling pity for his father's dilemma. "As time wore on, so did Dad's stamina. He didn't seem to have the original drive to fix up the place, although his love for it still showed. By the time I finished the first semester of my sophomore year, I was determined to stay here and help with things. I think Dad gave in, reluctant as his decision was, because he knew that under the circumstances, I had no more ambition about going to school than he did about remodeling the cabin. He knew that Mom needed him, and I knew that he needed me. So that was the end of that."

For the first time, Celia caught a glimpse of guilt

in the storyteller's face, but at the same time, a marked determination in the way he held his mouth.

"I could tell it wore Dad's spirit down that I was here instead of away getting the education he had always desired for me. But I assured him I could go back to school later, and made him a promise that one day, I would get that degree and hang it on the wall right over there," he said, pointing to the display of old photographs that Celia had noticed earlier.

At that point, she took a long, hard look at the pictures of his ancestors who had lived here before him. She made a note to bring her camera and add a picture of Donnie's family to that wall.

"Because that was my upbringing, that's why Anna and I are here. I hope, more than anything in the world, to someday give her and Bobby a fine home, and a life to be proud of. But for now, we are just trying to hold onto my family's old place. I can't stand the thought of seeing some money-grubbing banker buy it for not much of nothing and turn it into a bunch of houses with no personality and no meaning.

"We were doing okay, not great by any means, but we were comfortable," Donnie said, the words coming more slowly. He looked at Anna and stopped.

The guest could see his need to end with those words came more from not wanting to hurt his wife than from his own pain.

Anna picked up the conversation at this point. "Until I became great with child." She took Donnie's hand, letting him know that it was alright to say those words without feeling he had put the blame on her.

"It seems the school's insurance policy had some clause about my being employed there for a certain number of months before maternity benefits began," Donnie explained.

"And of course the insurance company from his old job wasn't about to pay for a baby born to someone who didn't work there anymore," Anna added, now a slight sadness in her voice.

"Anyway," Donnie continued, forcing a smile obviously for Anna's sake, "when the hospital and doctors found out about our situation, we had to have all the money paid before Bobby was born."

It didn't take Celia long to do the math. Her sister had given birth to a child ten years ago, and even then, the figures for the hospital and doctor were astronomical. She wanted to cry, or be mad, or something, but she didn't know what to do. For it didn't seem fair that these two people, who were trying so hard to make a decent life for themselves and their son, were having to suffer so much to have the things they wanted and deserved in life.

"After my sixth month of pregnancy," Anna explained, "I wasn't able to work any more. The doctors took me off my feet, so I was no longer able to help Donnie. We had been paying our bills on my salary, and the mortgage on his."

"Something had to give, so by the eighth month, I decided it had to be the utilities because I wasn't taking a chance on something being wrong with my baby or my Anna." Donnie smiled wistfully at his wife, the stress from seconds earlier gone.

The teacher's heart was again warmed, but not strangely this time. Here was a man who was extremely proud of his family and made no apologies for his deep love for them, and the decisions he made concerning them.

"I wanted to have a mid-wife come to the house. That seemed the proper way for our child to be born, especially with us living out here in this cabin and all, but after I wound up in bed for those last three months, Donnie wouldn't hear tell of it," Anna finished, her head bowed.

"I reckon there's some that would say I made some bad choices, but they're not in my shoes. My boy and my wife are both doing well, and I guess I'm just like my dad when it comes to that. There was no price tag on their well-being. And I couldn't let the farm go. I had a wonderful life here, and I want to see my boy do the same."

Donnie stopped here and took in a long, deep

breath, looking at Anna, the baby, then back to Celia. "I know it doesn't look like I've got much, Miss Brinkley, but as long as I'm here . . . with Anna and Bobby, I feel like I own the world."

Celia noticed that the rural dialect, absent before, had slipped its way into the conversation. In listening to this couple, she now imagined the great-grandfather, who had originally built this house, and his wife, after giving birth to their first child. There was something extremely nostalgic about their language now, as well as the dwelling. She could picture the members of the family who had lived and visited here, giving this home its distinct personality.

Talk about a place with an atmosphere, she thought dreamily, as she listened with both her eyes and ears.

"We're both very determined individuals," Anna added, again taking Donnie's hand, seeming to reassure her husband as much as herself. "I fully believe that one day, I'll even get to go back to college and be a teacher myself."

Celia blinked her eyes, and sat there speechless. Here was a man who could have easily lived in an apartment in town, and been, by most people's standards, comfortable, even on the meager salary he was receiving as a school's custodian. Yet, his love for family, tradition and old-timey values held him to this farm and the cabin, meaning that he would have a huge monetary challenge before him for many years to come.

And here was a woman, who in the face of all they did not have, and in the grimness of their present position, had a dream, an unrelenting hope of where she was going and what she wanted to do in life. Celia had never seen a stronger declaration or depth of faith. Both of these individuals had done with their future, totally and completely, what she had wished the teachers could do about Christmas earlier, and that was to leave it in the Master's hands.

This will make an even better human-interest story for the paper and newscast. The town can reach out to one of its own, someone whose family has been long-time residents of the county. Celia looked at Donnie's face, not full of strain, but rather strength, in his predicament. *And pillars of the community and salt of the earth,* she noted as an afterthought about the custodian's family. For it suddenly dawned on her that both the road sign beside the driveway, and the church just down the way, bore the name of this man's ancestors.

She stared into the dimness of the room, the faint images of the pictures on the wall barely visible in the flicker of candlelight. Celia closed her eyes, taking in all the beauty of her surroundings by using her other senses. There was an aroma, one that she couldn't distinguish, that she had never smelled before. There was an aura that could be felt in the air, one that was unfamiliar to her, but still clearly present, lingering for all who entered to experience. There was a peacefulness here that she had never known, even given all her years of living in solitude, void of many of life's stresses.

Celia, however, did know the source of that aroma, that aura, that peacefulness. It was love. Many, many years of love. Love that knew no end. Love that came down one Christmas. Love that came down that *very first* Christmas. And love that Celia had seen come down to the school and the community once again *this* Christmas.

She sensed she had been chosen as a special messenger, just like the Angel of the Lord on that first Christmas. It seemed her lot to tell the news of the birth of this precious child. It seemed her lot to spread the joy and glad tidings that came from being with this baby and his family. And it now seemed her lot to alert all in the village to come and see this child that had come to pass in their midst. The teacher felt completely caught up in the scene that so resembled the Christmas story, the same one she had heard for thirty-seven years.

CHAPTER 6

Driving back to town, Celia occupied the time of the ride by making a mental list of people she needed to call to help with her project. If she could at least get this couple on their feet, they both had the drive and initiative to make it the rest of the way.

Ah, life is good, she whispered to herself, thinking of how much richer Donnie and Anna seemed than she did. *What they're missing in some areas, they're sure making up for in others.* Celia smiled. *And they're sharing their riches with others,* she thought, realizing how much this couple had already blessed her. *And all the students that saw them today.*

Celia's mind was tinkering with ideas brought about by the story she had heard this evening. There was a lot more potential here than she had first realized. Anna wanted to be a teacher. Donnie had at least one year of college. They were both intelligent human beings who had turned to each other in a time of need. And now, there was no doubt in her mind that they were going to make it.

She couldn't wait to share this story with Dr. Lacey after the holidays. Celia knew there had to be some way they could make use of Anna, at least as a teacher's assistant or office helper. And surely they could help Donnie with some night classes at the local community college or university. The possibilities she envisioned were endless.

I'll plant the seed, and see which way it grows.

Celia walked into her home, determined to leave her newfound family to rest for this day, but she knew she had to do something to take her mind off that cold, dark cabin. After putting on a pot of water to boil, and opening a pouch of gourmet chocolate she had received the previous evening, she went to the bookcase and reached for last spring's yearbook.

She opened the front page and looked closely at the large picture of herself on the dedication page. It amazed her that the students had selected her for that honor. The gratitude she felt at that Friday morning's assembly program, when they made their presentation to her, came rolling slowly back to her mind. Celia knew the degree of talents and abilities possessed by all the other teachers of the school. Yet, she had the distinct privilege of working with every grade level, including all the preschool kindergarteners. And she did go out of her way to help each of the grades do their own special annual assembly program. So, in all reality, the reflective music teacher was given a golden opportunity to touch the life of each child that came through the doors of Tillman Academy.

Still, to have the members of the annual staff, the eighth graders who usually saw music as a slacker class, or one where the guys had grown past participation, Celia was well aware of the honor, and the appreciation, that had been bestowed on her by the students she cherished so deeply.

The musician eyed the picture closely. It was a good one. One that the photographer had loved, for he said it caught the way Celia spoke through her eyes. One that caught the openness of her mind - *through her eyes*. One that caught the love and deep concern for humankind - *through her eyes*. One that captured the energy and excitement that she felt each time she worked with the students - *through her eyes*. One that said she could be doing even more for the students, or for others, than she already was - *through her eyes*. And one that did *not* capture the loneliness she refused to admit from time to time - *through her eyes*.

How much have those eyes spoken to others in the past few days? Has anyone besides Mrs. Gaye seen the struggle going on - through her eyes.

Celia turned the pages, looking at every student, thinking of how she had observed each one grow and mature over her years of working with them, then recalling older siblings that had come through her classes in years past. The soul of the teacher couldn't help but think of all the many gifts these boys and girls held in their grasps. Gifts that could touch the hearts of many people. Gifts that were plain and simple and would cost nothing. And gifts that were easily within their reach to share without feeling any effort.

That final thought is what bothered the pensive teacher. She wanted the lesson she left with her students to have a lasting effect. An effect that would show them that the art of giving became most beautiful when the giver actually *could* feel the strain. A strain that left an impression that something had been given up in order to allow another to have something.

The families she worked with had all sorts of capacities right under their fingertips with which to help others. Continuing to leaf through the pages, Celia stopped when she came to the fourth graders. Looking closely at the faces of the boys who were a part of her ensemble, while imagining the pure, resonating sound of their voices from the night before, she began to think about all the possibilities that just these boys could offer to Bobby.

There was Jagdish, an Indian, whose deep, dark black eyes matched the blackness of his hair – the same black hair and eyes of his younger sister who melted the heart of Celia every time she looked at the child. Both children were graced with cherubic voices, which only added to the fact that they held a special place in the heart of the music teacher.

Their parents had come to this country to be educated and both were doctors. The mother was a pediatrician who spent every other summer in her native country teaching medical skills and working with advanced cases of illnesses and problems.

Her brain whirling, Celia was sure that one phone call would get little Bobby all the medical attention he needed. She pulled a tablet and pen from the drawer of the small table beside her chair and jotted herself a note to call the pediatrician's office first thing the next morning.

While she was writing, she also noted that the father was a general practitioner who could take care of Donnie and Anna, whenever the need arose. *That's two calls*, she boasted, proud of the way her list was beginning.

Next, she looked at the picture of Art, his perfectly round face and bright blue eyes that shouted that this boy was "full of himself," as Celia's grandmother's generation had called it. His blonde hair only served to accent the eyes and the playfulness of the child's character. The boy possessed a stocky build, all muscle, from the chores he did on his father's farm, giving him the appearance of a Swedish background.

Art, whose father owned the largest farm in the county, took great pride in helping with the animals. His goal was to be a veterinarian when he grew up, and take care of livestock for the farmers that were still left in the country, even though he knew he might have to move westward.

The father also owned the family business started decades ago, a farmer's supply and dry goods store that was more like the old-timey general mercantile shops. It carried everything from bibbed overalls to seeds, to candles for emergency lighting. She glanced over to the present Art had given her the evening before. *And the store also carries the best roasted peanuts in the world*, she mused, some of which the boy had brought to her in a huge bucket that could be used for an unusual flower-pot, or a prop for her upcoming production of *Oklahoma*.

There was no end to the list of things Art's father had at his fingertips that could be of use to Donnie on his own family's farm – items that would make a more productive life for Bobby.

Celia picked up the pen again.

Two of the other boys from the ensemble were shown next to each other in the yearbook. She looked at them and thought about their families, one whose parents were both attorneys, and the other whose father was a banker – next in line to the institution's president – and whose mother was a dental assistant. Both of these young men had most distinctive features, making them look the part of the line of established money and prosperous families from which they came. They also both played on the city's soccer team and had been selected as all-state players for the past two years. Yet, in spite of their many similarities in life, each of them had a much different outlook on life and the way they connected to the world, and others around them.

Lane, the child of the banker, had dark eyes, dark hair and a complexion that already gave him the appearance of a knock-out as a tall, dark and handsome young man. He was sure to have girls swooning all over him in his adolescent and college years, if not before.

And along with that endowment of good looks, this guy had also been blessed with a great personality and a sincere ability to reach out to others less fortunate than himself.

Celia could remember the look of joy, yet concern, in both his and his younger sister's eyes when they saw the baby in her classroom earlier that day. The teacher chuckled. *Yes, with that demeanor and those eyes, this guy, who's a natural-born charmer, is going to be a real heartbreaker when he grows older.*

The other boy, Drew, had a square chin and set eyes that spoke of old money from the get-go. He looked as if he belonged in a yachting club somewhere, like Boston, participating in a regatta rather than being in the fifth grade. Celia could imagine him, without any effort, in a dark-blue cotton sweater, complete with his family's crest, white slacks and dock shoes. His eyes carried that natural look of seriousness and competition.

A perfect trait for an attorney. It speaks for itself in the courtroom, she mused, making a note to look for those same eyes in his parents the next time she saw them.

Those same serious eyes were the ones that cued this boy's mind and voice to follow Celia's every direction during each performance. That was the trait she especially loved about him.

Drew was already set financially for life, and

didn't mind sharing that information with his classmates and teachers. Celia was appreciative that, in spite of the fact this student bragged openly about his possessions, he still had maintained the desire to achieve, to be someone in life, and not live off his accumulated stocks and inheritance. She did not see him ever being the prodigal son type.

She thought back to this morning and her kindergarteners. Drew's younger brother was in that class. He, too, had that impressive square chin, but his eyes had a softness that spoke compassion. This child had been the first in his class to actually reach down and touch the baby's tiny fingers.

Celia sighed, thinking of the individual traits that God gave each person, and how they chose to share those traits with others. Still using her creative insight, she thought of the gifts the families of these two young guys could offer. If things progressed as she envisioned, one of the attorneys could set up a trust fund for Bobby in conjunction with the banker, and this child could be provided dental care during his early years by the office for which Lane's mother worked.

Her hand was moving the pen quickly across the paper.

The teacher ran her fingers across the pages of the yearbook until she found one of the other boys. Rodney, who lived with his grandparents, was the spitting image of his debonair grandfather, with his long face, deep-green eyes and dark brown hair. His height and distinguishing features gave him the appearance of a miniscule man rather than a boy.

She thought about this child and, for the first time, wondered about his background. It had never crossed her mind to ask any of the other teachers about his parents. Not that she would have asked, respecting his privacy, but he wasn't the typical child who had been reared by grandparents. He didn't display any of the qualities of a "spoiled brat" that she sometimes saw in that type of home life.

Rodney exhibited a most pleasant disposition at all times. Manners came quite naturally to him, and he enthusiastically gave his best effort for her in class. For the first time, though, Celia's heart hurt for this child as she gazed at his picture.

While she sat there, staring into those eyes, she saw visions of Rodney's grandmother – a beautiful woman who had as much pep and vigor as herself. That woman was frequently at the school doing volunteer work in the office or helping in classrooms where she could. More than that, Celia saw the way the grandmother not only reached out with love for this child, but she disciplined him with that same love.

The teacher's sadness turned to joy as she realized what a blessing Rodney was for his grandparents, and they were for him. Thinking about it, she saw *nothing* missing from this child's life that was not in the lives of every other student at the school.

Huh! Celia grunted, *it's Rodney's artwork, selected from all the students' of the academy, which went out on the school's Christmas card this year.*

She looked at Rodney's picture one last time. *Nope, this guy has got it together. He has nothing to be ashamed of.*

Celia looked at the opposite page for the last of the boys in her ensemble. His picture looked exactly like Jody usually appeared – a face topped with disheveled, unruly blonde hair, but with a huge smile that would warm any heart, and bright blue eyes that demanded everyone's attention.

She couldn't help but laugh as she looked at this child. He drove every teacher mad, for he never appeared to be paying attention. Yet, if you questioned him on something from class, he could tell you verbatim what you had said – whether it be five minutes, five days, or five months ago. And more likely than not, he would add some detail the teacher had left out, because she didn't know it herself.

During one of last year's staff meetings, a teacher laughed about how he seemed to learn by osmosis. "Jody's like having an eleven-year-old absent-minded professor in the class," she had stated.

Celia, who felt she could respond to the comment honestly, being artistic herself, replied, "His father is a professor and his mother is an artist. What do you expect?"

He never did homework, but aced every test. And even when he wasn't paying attention, or so it seemed, he wasn't disrespectful. Every teacher loved him because of his sweet spirit that was constantly reaching out to others, and his unique sense of humor.

Unsurprisingly, Jody was the same for her. He daydreamed during class, but knew every song and action during performances. And his voice sounded like it had dropped down from heaven and fallen into this little boy. You never knew where his mind was during class, but when he hit the stage, he was on target.

The reminiscent music teacher reached to the table for the tin of cookies, one of the few food items she had kept for herself. As she replaced the lid after taking a couple of baked confections, Celia noticed the picture on the top of the container.

It was a reproduction of a 1938 Rockwell Christmas print from the cover of a *Saturday Evening Post*. In the picture stood five boys in little white choir robes with the oversized black bows, holding their music up, mouths wide open as they sang to the heavens. There were perfect examples of Lane, with his distinguishing features; Art, with his blonde hair and stocky Swedish build; Drew, with his dashing good looks (plus a black eye); and Rodney, looking all respectable like his grandfather. And there, in the front, stood the spitting image of Jody, saucer-sized eyes that were wide open, mouth in a perfectly rounded singing position, showing off his missing front tooth, blonde hair that looked like it hadn't been combed in a week, two band-aids crossed on his forehead, scratches on his fat cheeks, and hands lazily holding his music, with one short, stubby finger sticking out, all wrapped in worn gauze. The picture looked exactly like the child had come running in, had his robe thrown on him, and his music stuffed in his hand before being shoved onto the stage.

Needless to say, he's staring off into left field, Celia laughed, *which is probably where the child in this picture just came from.*

Replacing the container to the table, she eyed the tin's print long and hard as she was struck by the realization that even with their childlike qualities and natures, children possessed the purest of all voices. Voices that touched the spirit and warmed the soul, like the boys' ensemble singing *Gesu Bambino*. And she marveled at the way Rockwell had so appropriately, and simply, caught that fact in his artwork.

Celia flipped back to the dedication page. She slowly read the words that had been penned by the students of the yearbook staff who made the decision to honor her with the dedication.

"Tillman Academy has a special teacher who is responsible for the goodwill and "harmony" you find here. She gives of herself and her talents unselfishly. Her efforts on the Strawberry Festival, Christmas Programs, Musical, and planning for outside resources are always astonishing to all who are involved.

"She has been with us for the past eleven years and during all that time, she has worked with all grade levels on various performances. "The show must go on!" We will remember in our hearts that nothing will stand in the way of this lady and her love for her students. (Not even illness or the hospital.)"

Yeah, the hospital, Celia cringed, remembering being rushed to the hospital with internal bleeding on the morning of one of her annual Strawberry Festival concerts. Six hundred students were primed and ready for their best spring performance ever, and she was lying in the emergency room.

Luckily, the doctor on call had been a student's mother who understood the teacher's relentless plea to be released for the concert. Wanting to attend the concert herself, the doctor accompanied Celia to the school – once they had stopped the bleeding - and sat on the front row behind the stage, along with seven other students' fathers, who were also physicians.

The minute the concert was over, Celia was escorted back to the hospital. She remembered sitting on the piano bench, thinking how fortunate she was that she taught in a private school full of professional parents who cared so much about her well-being. *Reaping of the seeds I had sown in their children, no doubt.*

As she flipped the front of the book over to close it, a sheet of notebook paper fell from inside the front cover. Celia reached to the floor to retrieve it, wondering why she had stuffed it in her yearbook. She opened it to find a note from one of her students who had been a second grader at the time. The words, written in cursive with scratches through the mistakes, said, " Dear Miss Brinkley, Thank you for being the best music teacher in the world! Thanks for teaching me about Scott Joplin, Beatles, Elvis, how to sing better, to open your mouth wide, lots and lots of songs and tons and tons more!! You always make me smile when you twinkle your eyes. When you are feeling bad it make me sad because you don't twinkle your eyes as much. I'll miss you a bunch!" Following three rows of exclamation points, the child had closed, "Thanks for being great!" followed by another line of exclamation points. "Sincerely, Shelley Green" Music notes were drawn all around the paper with the letters "TY," short for "thank you," edging the border.

The music teacher recognized it as one of the many letters she had received during the weeks after the Strawberry Festival, while she was recuperating at home. *I'll be sure to put it with all the others tomorrow.* She knew that the note hadn't fallen out by sheer coincidence.

Instantly, Celia reopened the book, turning again to the dedication page. A word she had seen screamed at her now after reading Shelley's note.

No, dear child, the note wasn't coincidence. The thought rang so clearly in her mind that it was if it had come from above.

Celia read the words of the dedication, rushing to find the word that was now obsessively controlling her mind.

"Goodwill." That's the word.

Everything that was motivating Celia's current actions were catapulted by her desire to share goodwill. All the plans for Friday evening would be motivated by goodwill. The gifts from the community would come from people whose hearts were motivated by goodwill. Tillman Academy would hopefully become known for their goodwill.

And Celia Brinkley is the person responsible for that goodwill.

She stared at the words, staring back at her from the page where they lay in bold, black print, as she read them aloud slowly. "Tillman Academy has a special teacher who is responsible for the goodwill and "harmony" you find here. She gives of herself and her talents unselfishly."

Other words that were also in print made their way from her mind, where they had been committed to memory in second grade, to her lips as she recited them slowly. "And suddenly there was with the angel a multitude of the heavenly host praising God, and saying, Glory to God in the highest, and on earth, peace, good will toward men."

Goodwill. Her mind and her lips said the word at the same time.

Neither were the words of this dedication a coincidence, my child.

She bowed her head, now fully comprehending the reason for feeling "strangely warmed" the evening before. It was not the boys' voices, nor the glitz of the purple velvet curtain, nor the glow of the lights – *nor the baby's soft cry.* It was God using all those elements in culmination to speak to the heart of this servant, to call her to spread goodwill to Donnie and Anna . . . *and Bobby.*

Her heart, her soul, and her mind had been strangely warmed, calling her to submit herself – her talents - to a higher purpose. Celia Brinkley had been blessed with the opportunity to truly become as the Angel of the Lord, to spread God's message to the community to join their hearts in peace and good will toward their neighbor.

How is it that these students recognized this calling in me before I was aware of it myself?

A wave of humbleness literally ripped through her entire body, causing her to know that she had been ordained for a special job. Even in the words of the yearbook from last year, her task was documented, and now, in the comfort of her own home, the presence of the Holy Spirit was upon her, anointing her for this sanctified calling.

Oh, God, help me to be worthy of this job. Help me to bring honor and glory to Your Child through the work that we give for this earthly child. Help me to be Your instrument of peace and good will. And Lord, let your multitude of heavenly angels join their voices with the voices of these earthly children to proclaim your love for all *humankind.*

Celia closed the yearbook and held it close to her chest. In those pages were her children, her gifts from God, and the evidence of many years of giving of herself to those students. She imagined them in their warm houses, with all the modern conveniences life could afford, with their decorated trees, beautifully wrapped packages, and stockings all hung neatly in place.

And then she envisioned the candlelight, the old wood stove, the fireplace, and the warmth of two parents' love for a new baby. A tear trickled down the music teacher's cheek as she rallied in the truth that Bobby had the most important possession in all the world. *And it cannot be replaced by all the material things in my comfortable abode.*

※ ※ ※

Material things in my comfortable abode . . . material things in my comfortable abode . . . material things . . comfortable abode. Celia's body shook, urging her to get up and follow the message her mind was trying to send to her through her dream.

Her comfortable abode was full of boxes of material things that had been hauled off to the attic. One of those boxes contained something that she had forgotten, but obviously her subconscious had not.

Celia went into the back hallway and pulled down the attic stairs. As she climbed them, she was grateful that this was one item she had replaced since her move into the house. Otherwise, she would be standing in a chair trying to hoist herself into the attic.

The pull chain for the lights was barely within her reach, but she was able to grab it and cast enough light into the space to go on her scavenger hunt.

She rambled through the boxes, hoping to find what her mind told her was hidden away from her days of youth. For someone who was not a packrat, Celia found it odd that what she was searching for might be hidden in her attic; and if it was, she knew why.

Recognizing a box from her childhood, she pulled it out of its stack and brought it closer to the light. Carefully pulling the packing tape loose, she wondered if her effort would provide her any answers. The contents of the box included a diary, a locket, strands of hair from her first hair cut, music pins and recital programs, her old Barbie dolls, and a shoebox that had its edges taped shut.

Celia lifted the shoebox out from under all the other memorabilia. She knew that it housed a special part of her life. A part that had not been so important to her at the time, but as years had passed, a time that had held a great influence on her. She also knew that it was her mother who had the foresight to keep this box and the treasures it held, although probably not knowing why she did it at the time.

Placing the other items back in the large box, and putting it back in its stack, Celia took the shoebox down the steps and to the kitchen table, where she could lay its contents out in a neat exhibit. Knowing this could easily turn into a couple of hours' worth of memories and research, she opted to have another cup of chocolate while rummaging through the contents of the box.

Isn't it ironic, she mused as she boiled the water, *that so much of one's life and entire being can be placed in such a small container?* Celia looked at the box as if it were the object of some great archeological find, which to her, was exactly what it was. *And not only that, it's some old cardboard container that would have otherwise been thrown in the trash.*

Her thoughts turned to a carpenter's son, born in a lowly manger as she poured the water in her mug, another present from the previous evening. *Material things in my comfortable abode.*

Sitting down at the table, and reaching for the shoebox, Celia closed her eyes and let her mind drift back to the days of being a twelve-year-old, the same age as Jesus when he was found reading in the Temple. The age at which many religious traditions felt that a child had come "of age," and could be accepted as a member.

The magic moment had arrived. She opened the box and laid out the leaflets and the book and all the papers from her weeks of confirmation classes, looking for one particular piece of paper.

In searching for the description of John Wesley being "strangely warmed," her eyes ran across a paper where she had written his words for "The Rule of Life." She remembered sitting in the old hard wooden chair at a table, its height very uncomfortable for writing, as she copied from the board, "Do all the good you can, by all the means you can, in all the ways you can, in all the places you can, at all the times you can, to all the people you can, as long as ever you can."

A simple melody she had been taught with the words came to mind as she hummed it, then sang the words. *No wonder children remember everything they are taught to music,* she smiled.

Celia read over the words again. She loved their impact, yet their simplicity. Not wanting to disturb the papers from her confirmation, she grabbed a pen and paper and copied the words, *again,* so that she could use them with her classes after the holidays. *Fortunately, I remember the tune,* she thought, her fingers drumming out the notes on the table.

She pulled out a booklet that had a picture of John Wesley on the cover. *How pious he looks in that robe,* Celia observed, thinking how strange it was that he was the one whose evangelistic ways took his preaching out to the mines and fields rather than the pulpit. *Perhaps that's why he was "strangely" warmed!*

Scanning the pages, she found the heading that caused this search. Celia read every detail, trying to connect her feeling from the previous night to the one Wesley experienced over two hundred years before.

"Someone was reading from Luther's preface to the Epistle to the Romans, describing the change which God works in the heart through faith in Christ. I felt my heart strangely warmed. An assurance was given me that He had taken away my sins and saved me from the law of sin and death."

Celia had known God's presence in her life for many years. She was a believer, so she didn't think of last night as that moment when one feels Christ come into their heart. But what she did feel was the Holy Spirit's claim of her, of her life and her work.

And my acceptance of that call of the Holy Spirit, she whispered, thinking of the baby's low cry.

CHAPTER 7

$\mathcal{B}$rad rang the doorbell promptly at nine o'clock.

"We're not on the time clock this morning. You didn't have to be here precisely the second the clock chimed nine," Celia joked as she opened the door.

"I know. But I figured you're so completely organized that you'd be standing by the door waiting at ten till. And I also figured you'd take me for the sloppy, totally unorganized PE jock, so I wanted to give you the right impression to start with," the coach grinned, his radiant smile showing off his good looks.

"You mean you're *not* the sloppy, totally unorganized PE jock?" she asked, turning her head back slightly so that she was looking suspiciously at him out of the corner of her eye.

"Sorry to disappoint you, but I don't fit in that mold."

"Good, because when it comes to my personal life, I'm not the completely organized everything-down-to-the-tee individual, either. When it comes to anything besides my performances, I must admit that I'm the stereotypical artist who is always late and has everything thrown around in cluttered piles."

"So what's your excuse this morning?" Brad asked, peeking around to the immaculate foyer and living room. "You appear to be all dressed and ready to go. And I see no piles lying around anywhere."

"I made sure I was ready just in case there was an outside chance that you didn't fit the usual "dumb jock" mold," she answered, grinning back at him boldly.

Celia watched Brad raise his eyebrows as if he didn't believe her.

"Okay, so I happen to be overly anxious to get started with our project this morning," she conceded.

"That sounds more like a believable explanation," the coach said, helping her with her coat, and shutting the door behind her as they walked down the sidewalk toward his car. "Where to first?" he asked.

"How about the shops downtown? Most of the storeowners have children or grandchildren that are enrolled in the academy, or have come through our doors at one time or another. If not, they at least know of the school and will be supportive of our effort."

"You got it," he said, backing out the driveway, and heading down Union Street toward the downtown area. "How were you ever able to afford a house down here in the historic district on a teacher's salary?"

Celia glanced over at him with a broad smile. "I'm not like you. I couldn't depend on my good looks to get me any favors. So I had to depend on my friends."

"I'll take that as a compliment, . . . I think."

"Good, because that's exactly how I meant it."

Brad liked the playful twinkle he saw in the female's eyes. "And if I had to depend on my friends to get a house, I wouldn't have one," the coach added.

"So that's why you live in an apartment?" Celia asked, her tone letting him know that she was again kidding with him. But as she looked at the stoic silhouette of his face while he stared into the traffic straight ahead, she got the impression that he probably was pretty much of a loner. She hoped her comment didn't hit a wrong chord.

After the line of cars in front of them had turned off, he jumped right back into the conversation. "Great! I can tell this is going to be a fun day already," he laughed, joking back with her. "Now how did you *really* get the house?"

Celia inwardly breathed a sigh of relief at his jovial reply. "I really did have a little help from my friends. At the church where I attend, there was an older gentleman, who never married, that lived in the house. When he died, there were no children for him to leave it to, and his family didn't want the place. They're all very well-to-do, and have beautiful homes of their own, either on the golf course, or in the ritzy section of the historic district. And if you noticed," she added, leaning slightly toward him, "mine's the smallest house on the street."

She straightened her body back against the seat. "It so happened that I was looking for a small house at the time, and a lady in my church took it upon herself to ask if they might be willing to sell it to me. They were glad to get rid of it and I was glad not to have to go through a lot of hassle. Anyway, we agreed upon a price, I bought the house, and that's where I've been ever since."

"Isn't there a lot of upkeep with it being an older home?" he asked, concerned.

"Yes, I guess there is. But you have to remember, this guy was a bachelor who stuck completely to himself. He retired from a good job with the city, and he was the typical old fuddy-duddy who kept everything immaculate and in its place."

"Not a dumb jock, huh?" Brad smiled.

"Okay, enough with my wrong impression of you. Give me a break."

Oh, alright, if you insist, but just one."

Celia glared at Brad, with a look that told him she was having as much fun with this as he was. "Anyway, I was able to move into the house, most of it completely furnished. There were only a couple of small pieces that the family even wanted out of the house. I've changed a few things, installed gas logs, and tried to modernize it a little at a time, as I was able. But in answer to your question, no, I've never had anything catastrophic happen, knock on wood." And with that, she reached over and knocked on his forehead.

This time it was him who turned around and glared at her. "You think you're very smart, don't you?"

Celia knew that she was in for it. He would be waiting to get that one back at her. She knew she had best keep her guard up all day. It had been her style to surround herself with people who were as vibrant and enjoyed life as much as herself, and she could see that the day's choice of company was going to prove no different.

They spent the first half of the morning going from shop to shop telling each of the owners about the plan for Friday evening. Their main purpose was to make the shopkeepers aware that the school was requesting donations for the needy family, whether monetary or in merchandise, that either the parents or child could use. So they could cover more ground quickly, Brad took one side of the street, and Celia took the other.

It turned into a most profitable morning. They got everything from a new outfit for Anna and clothes for Bobby, to new furniture for the dining room. After they had visited every shop on Cabarrus Avenue and Union Street, the main business streets through downtown, they met back at the car to proceed to the next set of items on Celia's agenda.

"Where to now, boss?" Brad inquired, obviously enjoying this scavenger hunt as much as the woman in charge.

"Let's hit the offices of the utility companies," she answered, obviously with a detailed plan in mind. "They're just down a couple of blocks on Church Street. I surely hope the teachers made the calls yesterday afternoon so 'the powers that be' are expecting us."

"I suspect they were too afraid not to after the way you went into action on this mission. They didn't want the wrath of the mad musician on them when we get back in January!"

Celia simply shook her head and walked into the power company as hard and fast as she could.

❄ ❄ ❄

"That's one down," she boasted, as they exited the building.

"What did I tell you? The revenge of Celia Brinkley rings loud and clear on the heels of anyone who would dare to get in the way of her vision on this project."

"Oh, stop it. You make me sound like some evil doctor who has stepped right out of the pages of a comic book," she retorted defensively, trying to put on her best serious face.

They had already managed the few steps to the phone company next door, so the two rifling teachers held their tongues, not wanting to jeopardize their chances of sounding professional.

Celia knew the family that owned the phone company in this town also had many other credits to their name, one of them being that they were the initial benefactors of Tillman Academy. She felt sure if she played her cards right, this request would be a breeze, once the president of the phone company found out his generosity would put a positive light on the school. The prepared teacher also knew that this family had donated a pipe organ to the downtown sanctuaries of each denomination in the town, so they highly appreciated music. She hoped that her position at the school might count for something in her approach with the company's president.

She was right in her judgment. They walked out with another item on the list of contacts ready to be checked off.

"Okay, you've managed to get them three months of power and phone service. Now how do you propose to heat that place?"

"You'll find out as soon as you take me to the grill around the corner. Lunch is on me," she grinned, proud of her accomplishments, and walking off, not looking to see if the PE coach was following close behind her.

"Do you know I've never eaten here?" Brad asked, wolfing down a burger, complete with chili and slaw.

"Where have you been?" Celia asked, wondering how anyone, especially a single person, could live in their small town without patronizing What-a-Burger, a long-time Tillman establishment. "I'll bet you've never even eaten at the Red Pig, either, have you?"

"Okay, now it's time for you to give *me* a break. Just because my pad is on the other side of town from the school is no reason to crucify me," he answered, flashing her the same serious look she had tried on him only minutes earlier.

"Let's call a truce," Celia offered, wiping her

hand on the napkin before extending it to him for a shake.

"You've got yourself a deal!" Brad exclaimed, grabbing her hand and getting chili and mustard all over her fingers.

"It's just . . . well . . . where does a bachelor eat in this town if he doesn't eat at these two joints?" she asked, stumbling for a way to politely word her question, wiping her hand again.

"You'll find out when it's time for dinner," he replied, beaming that he had caught up with her quips.

"How was lunch?" Celia questioned, pointing to Brad's empty plate.

"You don't see anything left, do you? I might possibly consider letting you bring me here again sometime."

"Nope, next time we have to try the Red Pig," she corrected, obviously now also on a mission to acquaint this 'foreigner' to the places frequented by the locals. The music teacher decided to give him a list of Tillman's other hang-outs over the evening meal.

"What's next on our agenda?" Brad asked, holding the door for Celia to exit.

"We're going to make a stop at the hometown hardware store, the lumber company, the plumbing supply house, and the heating and air conditioning firm. I'd like to get Donnie some new items from those businesses."

"And I suppose you have contacts for all of those, too?" he asked, already knowing the answer.

"You betcha," she gloated. "And if everything has gone as planned, the teachers have already alerted those owners that we're on our way to see them today."

"You leave no stones unturned, do you?"

"Can't afford to in my business. Have you ever tried to do twelve productions a year on my budget?"

"No, I can't say that I have."

"Of course, you can't. The athletic department always gets all the money they need for their program."

"From the looks of that grand piano at the school, I'd say you get a hefty penny, too."

"I really can't complain," admitted Celia. "The parents have been wonderful to supply whatever costumes or props their children need, and there are always plenty of moms who are anxious to volunteer to do the sets and the scenery. It truly is a better situation than at most schools."

"But then from what I understand, you have a pretty good track record. The other teachers and Dr. Lacey obviously trust you and your work."

"I honestly have tried to do a good job for the school. We've had several accolades that have gotten the academy a lot of good publicity and exposure. The students are very talented."

"That's something else I've heard about you," Brad offered.

"What?" asked the musician, unaware of what he meant.

"You're too humble when it comes to your accomplishments. How many other teachers applied for that thing with the Met? And how many got chosen?" he pushed, trying to make her admit her worth to the school.

"I just got lucky," she blushed.

"Lucky, my foot. Is that why you were selected out of all those top musicians from around the country to be the composer for the entire group?" Brad stopped, taking Celia's hand and turning her body, forcing her to look into his eyes.

She looked at him sternly, wondering where he had gotten his information.

"Celia, everyone at the school knows that when you took your training with the rest of those fifty teachers, the instructors from the Metropolitan Opera chose you to be the composer out of the entire group. It was written up in several educational newsletters, not to mention the one from the Met. Why is it so difficult for you to see the good that you do, or admit that you're personally responsible for any of your successes?"

She started to walk away, but was pulled back. It had become clear that Brad was not going to let her get out of this conversation without an admission of her value to the school.

"What makes it impossible for you to take credit for anything you do?" he repeated.

The musician didn't know where to begin. "I guess I, too, have some complexes from my past," she said, more than ready to drop the subject.

Brad appreciated the fact that she didn't want to delve up memories that were a part of history right at the moment. He decided it was best to let her unleash those problems at the same time he disclosed his, later in the evening.

❄ ❄ ❄

"Pull in here," she said, pointing to a small dive off to the right.

"Tillman Creamery?" Brad asked, reading the letters on the side of the building. "This doesn't look like any air conditioning place."

"Nope, but it's plenty cold in the back of the building. I figure if you're going to live in this county, you need to get acquainted with all the hometown hang-outs."

They entered the front door and stood looking at refrigerated counters, full of different flavors of freshly made ice cream, that reached all the way across the room. Brad turned and looked behind him at the cases, filled with containers of fruit and grape punch, which lined the walls. Next to them stood coolers full of the standard fare of ice cream treats, and pint containers stacked all the way to the ceiling in the two tallest coolers.

"I've never seen so much ice cream in one place in all my life," he blared, surveying his choices like a kid who had just been turned loose in a candy store. "Which is the best?"

"I'm a die-hard butter pecan fan myself, but the coconut is really good, too."

"What are you having?" he asked, still trying to make up his mind as to what he wanted.

"I think I'll have my usual, a butter pecan milkshake," she answered, giving the woman behind the counter her order with the same sentence.

"One butter pecan milkshake comin' up!" blurted the server who had worked here since the founding of this place, back in the late thirties.

Celia suspected that the woman, who was barely a teenager at the time, had used that same bubbly voice since the day the doors first opened.

Brad got two scoops, one each of coconut and maple walnut, and stood with his personal tour guide outside the front door on the narrow sidewalk eating the frozen concoctions.

"So much for any kind of diet, huh?" Celia asked, scooping up the thick shake with a plastic spoon.

"Ah, go ahead, enjoy it. Diets aren't meant to

start until after the holidays anyway," Brad encouraged, not giving his double portion time to drip down the cone. "It seems funny to be standing outside eating ice cream in December."

"The creamery is a family tradition around these parts," explained the music teacher. If you drive by here on any summer night or weekend, you'll see folks of all ages lining this sidewalk, and piled two and three deep all along the side of the building."

"You know, this is why I like Tillman," he confessed. "It's the kind of community where you want to raise your kids."

"I wouldn't know," Celia laughed. "I'm too busy taking care of everybody else's to worry about any of my own."

Brad smiled back at her. "Yeah, me, too."

"Fact is, I've never really wanted kids," she continued. "And here I am working with them day in and day out. To top that, I wouldn't rather be doing anything else than working with those young minds. They're so impressionable, yet they're so full of thought." There was a slight pause, but her expression said she was not through. "Teaching is a way of staying young," she finished.

The PE coach could tell there was more to her statement, but it was going to have to wait until later to be heard.

CHAPTER 8

The line outside the restaurant wrapped all the way around the building. It was such a pleasant winter evening that the people seemed to enjoy waiting outside to be seated. Brad let out a whistle as he surveyed the number of customers already in line.

"Can you tell the Christmas shoppers are all out for last minute gifts?" Celia questioned.

"If they're all out for last minute gifts, what are all *these* people doing *here*?" Brad asked, continuing to estimate the number of couples in front of them. "Wait here," he instructed the music teacher.

He headed for the maitre'd's station to get on the waiting list. Celia wondered if he was the typical impatient male. Perhaps he had nothing better to do at home, so he would wait for a table and enjoy the evening out with some company, especially given it was a member of the opposite sex.

In only a matter of a few short minutes, Brad was back. He took the music teacher's hand and said, "C'mon."

"Where are we going?" she asked, as they walked past what seemed like hordes of other couples.

"Just follow me," he stated, pulling her along behind him through the line of people.

When they got to the door, a host took them to a table, handed them menus, placed their napkins in their laps, and took their drink orders.

"How in the world did you ever manage that?" Celia asked, her head still spinning from the treatment they had just received, as she watched the host walk away.

"Well, I guess maybe I do have *one* friend," Brad answered, his head buried in the menu.

"Who happens to be the maitre'd in this joint?" she quizzed, pushing his menu down with her hand so that she could see his eyes.

"Ummm . . . kinda," he smiled sheepishly.

"Ummm, kinda, my foot!" she shot, clearly teasing with him. "Don't give me an earful about having friends in high places who get things done ever again."

"Yes'm!" he grinned, putting the menu back up in front of his face.

Celia noticed him peeking at her over the top of it after she had a couple of seconds to stew. Neither of them said another word, but simply smiled at each other, enjoying the opportunity to sit back and relax in a gorgeously atmospheric surrounding. She heard strains of carols, played on a piano, a violin and a flute, coming from the adjoining room.

Seeing her listening toward the direction of the music, Brad asked, "Would you have rather been seated in the room with the piano?"

"No, this is perfectly fine. This way, we won't have to scream over the music at each other to be heard."

"I'm glad you feel that way. I figured you're like most musicians who don't want their precious voices to be near the smoking section."

"And exactly how did you know that?"

"I did go to college, Celi, and face it, you musicians do have a pretty notorious reputation."

He called me Celi again. Brad had called her that once before during the afternoon, shortly after their visit to the creamery. This time she was sure it was no accident. A ripple ran through her as she realized the ease

143

he must feel in her presence. Did she dare tell him that was the pet name her grandfather had for her? She decided to wait and see how the evening progressed. But for now, she decided to change the mood – *quickly*.

"Brad, how long has it been since you've seen your father?" Celia asked, taking up a conversation he had begun on their drive here.

"I was fourteen. We grew up in a very high society setting. That's why I was introduced to golf and tennis at an early age. Father was determined that his son would excel and be better than all the other kids whose families belonged to the country club.

"In that ring of people, he was a social drinker. After I was old enough to really have any knowledge about things, I saw that the alcohol was becoming a problem. He wasn't his old fun-loving self any more. All he ever did was scream at us . . . and his friends, too."

Celia noticed the cheerful look in Brad's eyes turn to one of sorrow as he spoke.

"I don't know how long he'd been out of work before Mother finally told us kids that we were broke, that Father had lost his job. Yet, he continued to spend what was left as if there was a never-ending stream of money. He didn't want his friends to know about his state of affairs, so he kept up the lifestyle he had created for himself until he had finally gone through every penny we had.

"Mother didn't even have money to go to the grocery store anymore. She retreated, trying to stay away from friends and family, denying what was going on in front of her eyes."

The music teacher noted the stress in the coach's body from his hands, clamped together, which he was squeezing as he spoke.

"Once the money was gone and we lost our home, she still tried to pretend things would get better. I think in her mind she knew otherwise, but her heart told her to try to hold on to her belief in Father. That went on until one day, when she came home from the salvage shop where she wound up having to buy outdated cans of food, and found that my younger brother, Eric, had been severely beaten. Beaten so badly, in fact, that we had to take him to the hospital. Of course, we had no insurance at that point, so he wound up being an indigent case, which terribly humiliated my mother – especially when the nurse who tended to Eric had been one of her best friends."

Brad's eyes looked directly into Celia's at this point. "But when it came down to choosing between my brother's well-being, and her pride, Mother said there was no choice. She had taken me with her to the hospital. We had to take the bus because the cars had both been repo'ed. I stayed with my mother night and day at the hospital until Eric was discharged. I can remember sleeping out in the lobby, while she never left his side. She caught what few winks she did with her head on the edge of his bed, or either in the straight-back chair beside it. We had no place to go, but she was determined not to go back to my Father after that."

He took a deep breath and sighed heavily. "The nurse who knew my mother helped us get through that period in our lives. It just so happened that she had a sister, in another town, who could give Mother a job. We were able to find a small basement apartment close to our school and Mother's work, so that's when I learned there really *was* a God. I felt Him smiling down on us, in spite of our horrible station in life.

"What really hurt about the entire ordeal was the fact that Father never even knew where we were, or tried to find us. He was so drunk when we left with Eric that he didn't even know we were gone until who knows when."

His lips pursed as he continued to speak. "I wanted to hate him. I wanted *desperately* to hate him. But after feeling like God had enabled us to get away and find a safe place, and Mother got a job, I was afraid. I feared that if I hated my father, God would take away all the things He had provided for us.

"The first year was a terrible struggle, but we managed to get through it. We never heard from Father, and to my knowledge, Mother never asked around to see how he was." Brad sighed again. "It was easy to see that she was broken-hearted about her perfect storybook marriage turned inside out. But her responsibility to her sons must have meant more to her, for I never saw it get her down to the point of not giving us the best she could."

Celia saw a slight smile take shape on Brad's face.

"After that, I got a job and helped out as much as I could. Mother swore to pay back every penny I gave her, but I felt great satisfaction in being able to be the man of the house and pull part of the load. I did well in school and at work. The principal somehow found out about what was going on with me, so he took me under his wing and made sure I got all sorts of opportunities for odd jobs, then later scholarships.

"He even encouraged me to get into the auto mechanic class, where I was able to rebuild a second-hand car, and have it. It seemed like if I kept taking care of what God gave us, He kept on smiling, and kept on giving." The PE coach paused and appeared to be reminiscing about those days from his teenage years.

"Mother was, and still is, a beautiful woman. She got offers for dates, but she never took them. I suppose she could have gotten remarried, but I really think she never wanted to pursue the divorce, simply because she didn't want to have any kind of contact with my father."

Brad shrugged his shoulders. "Anyway, now he's in a group home. Eric and I asked some of our friends from the old neighborhood and found out that much. The alcohol finally affected his mental health as well as his physical health, from what I understand. I'm not even sure who or what he knows, and frankly, although my mind was made up not to hate him, the truth of the matter is, I really didn't care. I dismissed him totally from my thoughts."

Celia felt such a rush of emotions that she was unable to speak. The silence seemed to give both of them time to reflect on their pasts, people who had hurt them, people they needed to forgive, and time to hurt for each other.

❄ ❄ ❄

Dinner was magnificent. Celia was impressed that Brad had brought her to a place that was new to her. She was more delighted that the shrimp alfredo was as good as the service of both their waiter and the maitre'd.

As should have been the case, the time of confessions came to a close when the food was served, but the music teacher wondered if Brad still had something he wanted to unload from his chest. The day's accomplishments told her she could feel safe in his presence, so she ventured to make an invitation that she would have never dreamed of with any other man after knowing him for such a short while.

"Brad, would you like to come in and talk when we get back to my house?"

She could see the immediate relief on his face. "Thanks, Celia, I guess my anxiousness shows, doesn't it?"

"A little," she answered, thinking how odd it was for a man so strong, and who gave off such a positive image as Brad, to show intimidation in talking about any subject, painful or otherwise.

"Celia, not only haven't I seen my father in years, I've not spoken to anyone about him, or even allowed myself to broach that subject internally." There was an apologetic expression on Brad's face as he spoke the words.

She looked longingly into his eyes until she was sure she had his attention. "Brad, do you ever stop to pray for him, or about him?"

"Oh, I'm sure I do. Isn't God supposed to know what's on our hearts, and in our minds?"

"Yes, he is. But prayer is a very powerful tool. In order to get the most from it, I believe one must consciously spend time, deliberately, with God. Maybe it's just the way I was raised, but I really believe that God will truly bless those who are always anxious to offer Him thanks and praise, as well as come to Him in times of need.

"I wouldn't know how to start my days if I didn't say, 'Good morning, God' and thank Him for allowing me to spend another day on earth in His presence." She paused briefly as a small smile came across her face. "Maybe it's just because I'm single and live alone, but I relish each moment that I'm alive. I see it in two ways. One, I can be useful to someone else, and two, there's something else here on earth that I haven't done or enjoyed yet." Celia was glad to see Brad's watchful eyes. "So I try to make the most of every day."

She decided that was enough of a sermon for one evening, so the music teacher stopped before she scared away her guest. But to her surprise, he picked up the conversation.

"Celia, I believe in God. I truly believe in God. In fact, as a high school graduate and early college student, I wrestled with going into the ministry." Brad felt an instant relief that there was no look of shock on the face sitting across the table from him. "I know a large part of that desire came from wanting to help others who had to face what I had gone through with my father and my own family."

"Brad, you do know that's a very common reason for people going into any profession. They've been down a road, a terribly painful road, and it leaves them with the yearning to make sure others don't face the pain, or make the same mistakes that they did. Look at all the self-help books on the market today. Years ago, people didn't talk about personal problems. But now, they not only talk about them, they use their stories and their backgrounds to help others deal with the same garbage in life.

"I can remember when I was in ed psych classes in grad school," Celia recalled. "The professor made a statement to the effect that if you look at kidney specialists, someone in their family probably died from a kidney disease. He said the same holds true for many heart doctors, cancer doctors, you name it. There's very likely a hurt present somewhere in the life of those doctors."

The two sat quietly looking at each other for a few minutes as the waiter cleared their table. Brad digested Celia's words, while Celia wondered if Brad was meant to be something other than a coach. She secretly prayed for his ease in taking control of the plight with his father.

Thank God for waiters with delectable dessert trays, Celia thought as their silence was broken by the man standing beside their table with a vast array of sweets. Although she was not usually into desserts, the moment seemed to call for something to give this pleasant dinner, the encore to a day of helping another in need, the ending it deserved. Brad obviously thought the same thing by his interest in the tray's offerings.

"Okay, Celi, you go first. Then I'll get something else and we can share."

"Ooh, a man after my own heart," she said, like a child shrieking with delight.

Then her choice of words hit her. She hoped she had not said anything that would be taken as flirting. Brad had seemed to open up to her, to trust her. Right now he needed a friend, and she didn't want to do anything to destroy a relationship that was building in that area for them.

Suddenly, the impact of what he had called her, for a third time, sank in. "Celi." Did this man, in his excitement over the desserts, leave out a syllable, or had he become that confident and comfortable with her friendship? She added a sentence to her earlier prayer, hoping it was the latter.

As the couple finished the last bites of their praline cheesecake and double decadence chocolate cake, they lifted their glasses in a toast to a most profitable day. And both uttered a silent prayer, hoping that the evening would bring one more blessing, one of relief for Brad in his memories of the past.

❄ ❄ ❄

"This house has a lot more room than it appears from the street," Brad surmised as Celia gave him the grand tour of her home.

"Yes, it goes back on the lot rather than across the road front. I guess the guy that built it wanted a lot of privacy. It suits me just fine."

"But where's all the mess you mentioned earlier? I don't see any unorganized piles stacked in any of the rooms," he teased, recalling her comment from the morning.

"It's pretty hard to make a big mess when you live alone. And not only that, this is the time of year that I'm rarely home. Too much going on at school. But give me a good week at home by myself, with a little time to start several new projects, and *voile!* – one big mess."

Brad laughed, and shook his head. "Celia, you moved into this home after a bachelor. Are you going to stand there and tell me there weren't piles of clothes and dirty dishes setting around when you bought the place?"

"No, actually there weren't," she answered thoughtfully. "Of course, I'm sure the guy's family had cleaned the place up before I saw it, but it was immaculate from the first time I stepped foot in it. Once they found out I was interested in it, and we agreed on the price, it was basically a matter of them going through all his personal effects while my loan went through. As I said, most of this furniture was his."

The PE coach looked around. "Some pretty fine furnishings for an old geezer."

Celia laughed at his response. "Yeah, that's what I thought. But it seems that when he built the place, he had his sister-in-law to have it decorated so he wouldn't have to mess with the hassle. She's the prim-and-proper type, so he got what she'd have picked out. I guess it didn't much matter to him, as long as he had a place to park his behind, and rest his head."

"You're too much," Brad grinned.

"What?" Celia asked, defensively.

"Don't take offense. It's just that you somehow don't fit the mold of what I would've suspected from you."

"Well, you're not exactly what I had you pictured as, either!" she said with a sideways glance. "Could I get you some coffee or hot tea or chocolate?"

"A good cup of black coffee sounds great," Brad accepted.

"Regular or decaf?" Celia stopped and looked at him. "Never mind. You don't look like the ultra-health freak."

"I'll have you know that I once trained for the

Olympics." Now it was his turn to be defensive. "I was an unstoppable tennis player. Unstoppable, that is, until a knee injury ruined my movement and agility. I can still play, but nowhere near Olympic quality."

"I'm sorry, I didn't know," Celia offered apologetically.

"It's no big deal. I just figured it wasn't supposed to be and made my mind up to be content with being a PE coach. That had been a back-up plan anyway after I decided the ministry wasn't for me."

"I never asked at dinner, but how did you get from wanting to be a minister to becoming a PE coach?" she asked, her intrigue showing.

"Even if I had gone into the ministry, I wanted to be a youth pastor, so the desire to work with kids and young people had been there from the beginning," explained Brad. "Since I was good at sports, especially golf and tennis, PE seemed a natural way to come in contact with teenagers every day. I had actually planned to work in a middle school, or high school, but when the Tillman job came open in this area, I figured it was a Godsend. This is where I wanted to live."

"Do you have any family here?"

"No, but my mom and brother are only a couple of hours away. Tillman is near a big city that has all the sports arenas, but it's still away from the traffic and has a country feel to it, so I looked for a job in this area,"

Brad reasoned. "I can get right on the interstate from my apartment and be home with my mom in no time."

Celia walked out of earshot as she reached the kitchen. A few minutes later she returned with a tray of homemade cookies and after-dinner coffees and hot chocolates.

"That's quite a spread for someone who lives alone. You must entertain a lot."

The music teacher thought she caught the edge of a question to Brad's statement, a fact that slightly excited her. She didn't know why, but she was pleased that he seemed to care.

"No, I don't even drink coffee, but during the Christmas season, I happen to get inundated with all sorts of gourmet beverages. You'd get the idea that those yuppy parents think all I do is sit at home with a cup of expresso in my hand."

She caught a brief chuckle from Brad.

"Well, you must admit, it does fit your type," he said, giving her a mock explanation.

"Yes, I guess so, but we've already put the case to rest that I don't fit my type any more than you do," Celia reminded him. "Besides, don't tell me you don't get all those baskets full of goodies. You know, the ones that sit around until time for the next school year to start, at which time you throw them out in the mad dash of getting cleaned up and organized for a new beginning." Her eyes searched for the slightest glimmer that he knew exactly what she meant.

"Sorry, but no, I don't. They give me all sorts of athletic gear, socks, you name it. If it has anything to do with sports, I get it."

This time it was Celia's turn to chuckle. "And that fits *your* type."

"Or not," he smiled back at her. "What no one has discovered at the school is that there is a lot more to me than being a single "jock." If the truth be known, I spend my time reading non-fiction, usually books with a lot of depth to them." He paused, looking at Celia with a most serious expression. "And if more of the truth be known, I'd kinda like for them not to know that."

"Why?" she questioned. "I should think you'd like them to know there's a lot more substance to you than some overgrown high school ball player."

"That's the beauty of it. If they knew my background, that I nearly went into the ministry, the students might not trust me the way they do now. Especially the middle school and high school guys. They look up to me, for several reasons. But if they realized that in the back of my mind, I was constantly looking and listening for ways to make a difference, or an impact on an area of their lives where they were hurting, or lacking something on the home front, they wouldn't respond to me the way they do." Brad looked to see if she understood. "Do you catch my drift?"

"Brad, don't you think that every one of the academy's teachers wants to make a difference in the lives of our students? For that matter, I believe every teacher in the world ultimately enters that profession for the purpose of shaping young lives."

"Perhaps you're right. But in my last job, it seemed that the most experienced teacher had lost that zeal, that desire." A pained expression came over Brad's face as he continued. "I made a vow never to get to that point of burn-out. Or reach the day that my sole purpose for walking in that door was to get a paycheck, or keep my insurance, or increase my pension."

Celia despised what she was hearing in Brad's voice. As badly as she hated to face it, those were the very same sentiments with which she had been dealing, along with the feeling that she could be doing more for those who needed her worse. Her conscience began its own private battle of whether this was the reason she wanted to leave the teaching profession. Was it merely a crutch for something she really didn't want to admit, even to herself? Was Brad speaking the very same words that were locked inside her?

The music teacher realized that her face mirrored the exact pained expression she saw on the man sitting across from her.

Brad could tell that his honesty was putting a

damper on the day that had been so rewarding. He knew the subject he was about to approach wouldn't serve to be any better, but at least it would get their minds veering in a different direction.

"Enough of my idle thoughts. It's time for a confessional from Miss Celia Brinkley."

"What sort of confessional?" she asked, not sure she really wanted to know.

"I've told you the deep dark secrets of my past. Now it's your turn to tell me why it's so difficult for you to take any credit for any of your accomplishments."

Celia shrugged. "It's really not any deep, dark secret. It's just that . . . when I was growing up, my older sister was the apple of my dad's eye. As far as he was concerned, she could do no wrong. Not once did he notice anything that I did." The musician looked down at her feet. "I can remember hearing my mother behind their closed door at night telling him that maybe it would be a good idea if he sometimes said any kind words to me."

Brad began to wonder if he was putting an even darker ending to their day of promises.

She looked back up, letting her eyes meet his. "You know what his response was?"

The PE coach shook his head, allowing her to continue revealing this obviously hurtful time from her childhood.

"I can still remember burying my head in my pillow to muffle the tears as I heard him tell my mother that he never wanted me anyway. That she was the one who wanted another child, a 'baby to coddle' he mocked, 'cause you say I'm always giving my attention to Beth. I told you then I never could, and never would, love another child like my little girl, my Beth. So, as you wanted, you keep to your little girl, and I'll keep to mine.'

"When I heard my mother's tears, I felt even worse. She had been so good to me, and so careful not to show any partiality between Beth and me, and I knew that Daddy's comments pained her greatly. His words, combined with her tears, made me feel I had betrayed her, and I began to place what has continued to grow into an escalating pile of guilt on myself for that pain." Celia's eyes showed sympathetic tears for her mother.

"I'm sure she had no idea that I heard every word. I didn't mention it to her, ever, but I could tell afterwards that she made a point of trying to protect me from being around my father. She'd habitually find fun chores for me to do with her, or let me stay with friends. In fact, I think that's why I was allowed piano lessons. It was like she was willing to provide me with an escape, something that would remove me from the reality of being an unwanted child."

Brad felt badly that he had opened an old wound,

one that had apparently scarred over. He first wondered if perhaps this would cause it to pour forth the poisonous venom of a moral infestation all over again. But he saw instead a lightening of the pain in Celia's face, and reasoned that maybe he was the sounding board she had desperately needed. Perhaps this conversation would prove to be a complete and healthy release that would lead to a long overdue resolution between her and her father.

He loved the glow of her inner spirit, one that still showed in the midst of reliving a stormy time of her life. His ears caught him up with the sentences he had missed while watching her face. Then Brad realized that her words had stopped, and that she was looking into his face with the same intensity with which he was staring at her.

"I'm sorry," she apologized. "I didn't mean to bore you."

"You didn't bore me at all. I just wondered if I had pushed you into a corner where you didn't want to be."

"No," Celia shook her head slowly. "I had not relished the idea of talking about this. But I guess after listening to you earlier, I felt comfortable enough to allow my vulnerability to show. In fact, if I'm going to be going into another field – one where I want to be able to reach out to others – I have to be able to let them see that my life hasn't always been a bed of roses, either."

"I think you're right," Brad replied. "It's a lot easier to trust someone when we feel some common ground with them."

"There is more to the story . . . if you're interested," Celia offered, not wanting to belabor her listener.

"Of course I'm interested, Celia. Please don't feel embarrassed by anything you want to say. Remember, I nearly became a minister. I like being able to help others open old wounds and allow the poison to drain."

She nodded, continuing with the story, but in a softer tone. "During Beth's senior year in high school, she became pregnant. Father was crushed. He forbid her to see the baby's father, saying that 'no boy, especially one still in high school, was good enough for his darling.' Daddy made our mother take care of Beth, and he refused to talk about the child developing inside her body. As she became increasingly larger, he got to the point he wouldn't even come to the dinner table, and he left each morning for work before she got up and moving. I'm sure the situation caused more strife between he and my mother, for I didn't hear them speak to each other at all for at least a couple of months."

Her pained expression returned. Brad could tell it was not for herself, but for her loved ones, as Celia's voice matched the look on her face.

"The child, a son, was stillborn after almost eight

months. My father couldn't bring himself to come home for dinner for over three months after that. For whatever reason, my parents managed to get through a terribly stressful time, mainly because I think my mother knew better than to try to console, or even talk to my father. She stayed completely clear of him. Her lead proved to be the example that I needed to do the same."

Brad recognized the fumbling of her fingers, as Celia looked at her hands, as a way to give her the strength to finish the story.

"Poor Beth had enough of her own grief. She turned against our father, and I can't say that I blame her. At that time in my life, I'm sure I would have reacted the same. To this day, I don't think that Beth has ever completely forgiven him. And it's pretty clear, through his obvious misery, that he's not forgiven himself, either."

Celia paused and sighed as Brad moved over to the chair and sat beside her on the overstuffed armrest. She could read his body language, which said he shared her sorrow, and that he was there should she need a shoulder on which to rid herself of a few tears.

As she continued to speak, he wondered if it was from strength, or sheer desire to get this out of her system once and for all. Relentlessly, the music teacher headed toward the end of her story, not seeming to need his comforting strength *or* shoulder, but appreciative for the offer of both.

"Holidays seem the most strained," she said, a shakiness now in her voice. "I think that Mother and I have both managed to move forward, and I try to help her make the most of the times when we're all together. But her eyes still show that there are many hidden tears behind them . . . I believe for both Beth and Daddy. And even though she hasn't ever mentioned it to me, it's clear that she's never stopped praying that one day a healing would come.

"She's such a wonderful wife and mother, from great European stock, that I think those are simply inherent qualities in her. Even though she is the fairer sex, and my father looks the part of the rough and tough Norseman, it's she who's held what little family ties together that there have been over the past fifteen years.

"It's her simple style to make sure that Daddy, and everyone else, understands her submissive position in the family. But at the same time, it's amazing how demanding her demeanor is, for I'm sure it's for her benefit that no one ever mentions the past, letting it go as if it didn't happen."

Celia stopped and looked into Brad's eyes. The depth of his gaze suggested that he was right along with her in the conversation, listening intently to whatever she wanted to tell him. But as she sat there, now silent and motionless, he had to ask a question that had been pacing back and forth in his head during the past several minutes.

"Do you think that perhaps it would help the healing process to begin if your family sat down together? Not with Beth's spouse or children, but with you and your mother, alongside of Beth and your father, and someone took the initiative to move gently into a conversation that could allow a liberating forgiveness for one of them. Surely if one began to break down the barrier, they could somehow find a way to meet in the middle."

"I agree that we need to talk . . . or at least Beth and Daddy need to talk. And I'm sure that would be a lot easier if Mother and I were there for moral support. I even feel like Beth could get to the point that she could apologize to Daddy for the years of pain." The music teacher stopped and looked squarely into Brad's eyes. "But you know what really hurts more than anything?"

Brad continued to sit on the armrest of the chair, looking at Celia, unsure whether to physically nod, or simply let his eyes give her a silent answer.

"It really hurts that I'm afraid Daddy would never accept Beth's apology, or even try to meet her in the middle. I'm afraid he would leave her out there, completely vulnerable, left hanging to dry without even a word of encouragement for her brave efforts."

Celia sat there, searching the coach's face for even

a glimpse of understanding.

"And just as importantly, I feel he owes Beth an apology, too, which will probably never come."

Brad sat stunned. Here this woman, who harbored no jealousy toward a sister who was wanted and favored over herself, saw a need for an apology for the sister, but not for her own self. What love she must have learned from the mother.

As if reading his mind, Celia concluded with one final thought. "Do you know what's struck me as most peculiar, or should I say amazing, as I've matured into an adult? It's the realization that I've never hated my father for his words. Even through the hurt I felt, not only knowing he cared more for Beth, but hearing him say it, I knew I still had Mother. And I knew that was more than some children had. Instead of hatred, I felt a sorrow for Daddy, for he was incapable of seeing the love I had for him."

Celia shrugged. "I guess it was easier for me to excuse it that way, knowing the lack of love from him. Had I been loved by both parents, it probably wouldn't have meant as much to me. It's that same old thing of taking little things for granted . . . we don't tend to appreciate things when we have them." She stopped, letting her thoughts drift back to her childhood, and the early years when she had looked up to her father.

Brad saw in this co-worker a longing to fix a

problem. He felt a desire to fix it for her. And he shared the knowledge that no matter what either of them wanted for their own individual situation, both of their sets of circumstances were out of their control – *except for one thing!*

Brad took Celia's hand and led her from the chair to the sofa that sat opposite the fireplace. "I think we've both made it clearly evident that we're not ashamed of our spiritual beliefs, and that in the past couple of days, we've come to appreciate that quality in each other. We've already seen the blessings reaped from our prayers of yesterday with the other teachers. Would you like to be prayer partners, to use our combined efforts for the good of these shortcomings and misgivings on behalf of each other and our families?"

Celia stared at him and nodded. Her eyes looked past him, into the open space, as she expressed a thought that ran through her mind. "I know there are some faiths that believe a person can only pray for their own needs. But it seems to me, in times like these, that one's heart becomes so heavy, and hurts so much for a loved one, that our thoughts and sentences don't express to God what we want them to. I know that He doesn't need to hear our words.

"I guess that what I'm trying to say is I've always been so adept at expressing myself exactly as I wanted, through my words and music, that I still feel that's necessary when talking to God. You're the first person who's ever offered to sit with me and express the concerns of my heart *for* me, when I was unable to do it for myself."

Brad placed his hand on her thin shoulder. "Celia, have you ever shared this past, or even thought about sharing it, with anyone so they *could* pray with you about it?"

Her eyes told him what he wanted to know. Brad could see that he'd not made a new discovery here for the music teacher, but rather that she'd chosen to suppress it from herself and others. Like him, it was easier to go through the day-to-day living without dredging up the pains from the past.

All of a sudden, it struck Brad as to the healing that could come if they were both able to face, completely face, their past hurts, and how much more of an asset they could each be to their students and their professions if they could move past the hump that had been in their paths for several years – in fact, about the same number of years.

"Celia, have you ever thought that maybe this scar is keeping you from attaining your full potential in reaching out to others?"

She looked at Brad with an odd expression, an expression that slowly grew into a look of admiration and appreciation. It was as if his lips had just spoken of something that had been buried inside her for years, something of which even she was unaware, for it was hidden so far in her subconscious.

The ringing of the phone lightened the air. Having a hunch it could be a call about the next evening's nativity, Celia moved quickly to answer it.

"Miss Brinkley, this is Stan Myers, Art's dad."

She recognized his voice from the evening before when she had called to ask him to furnish a heater, a manger and animals for the event.

"I hope I'm not calling at a bad time," he continued, "but I just now read your note that went home with the students about tomorrow night."

Celia pushed the button for the speaker phone so that Brad could hear the conversation, also.

"No, it's a perfect time, Mr. Myers. What can I do for you?"

"It's more of 'what can I do for you?' or rather, for the Little's. When I read the note, I realized that Donnie Little's family has been doing business with my family's store for generations. In fact, they've carried an open account with us for years, since right after that cabin was built. I had no idea that Donnie worked at the school. That man comes from fine stock, and I'd like to do whatever I can to help that family."

The look of excitement on Brad's face matched the one on Celia's. He moved closer to the phone to make sure he didn't miss the generosity of the caller.

"Put me down for a year of no statements on anything. You tell that man just to come in and get whatever he wants anytime he needs something. I'll make a note in the computer."

"Yes, sir," Celia glowed. "I hope you'll speak to Donnie yourself. I'm sure it would mean a lot to him."

"I sure will," came Mr. Myer's energetic response. "My father thought very highly of Donnie's grandfather. And I'd like to thank you for doing this for him and his wife and baby. We never know when any of us could be struck by some hardship, wiping out everything we own."

"That's true. And thank you for this generous offer. I'm sure it will be greatly appreciated," the music teacher concluded, her voice expressing her own appreciation.

Celia radiated as she hung up the phone and turned to Brad. "We've come a long way, baby. Can you imagine what Donnie's great-grandfather would have done if they had keyed his purchases into a computer?"

Brad shook his head as he gave Celia a high-five. "Chalk up another one to Celia Brinkley."

But as the words came out, he knew as well as his co-worker that she had nothing to do with what was going on around them. They were both tiny pieces of a bigger puzzle, a greater plan.

Their conversation made its way back to the successes of the day, and the work still to be done before the nativity the next evening. "You know," Celia thought out loud, "I hope that cabin doesn't lose its charm and personality in the process of all the upgrades."

"You can't worry about that, Celia. Houses get old and run-down, and improvements must be made or they will fall to the ground. There's upkeep with any property."

"I know you're right, Brad, but that house is so full of love and memories. So much of what is there isn't even structural. I wish you could see it before you leave for the holidays."

"I'll go by there tomorrow morning. I may not be able to feel or experience what you have by being there, but at least I can see the place."

"That would be great. Why don't you stop in and speak to Donnie and Anna? And maybe drop by with a present so you don't look too suspicious? You can tell them I gave you the directions. I'm sure they won't mind."

He nodded. Brad knew that the confessions of the evening, while unloading some of the baggage that had been carted around for years, had taken an emotional toll on both of them. Excusing himself, he wanted to allow Celia some time to reflect on the past, now that it was finally back in the open. He was sure they would resume their discussion the next evening after the nativity, or at some point during the holiday vacation. And he knew this was only the beginning of many conversations between them.

CHAPTER 9

Brad slipped quietly through the door and made his way around the back of the classroom where he could watch Celia working her magic with the children. While the boys and girls trickled into the large music room, each carrying a special gift they had brought for Bobby, he couldn't help but notice the way she greeted the students, giving each one a hug that said she loved them as her own. While the last of the middle schoolers were getting robed in their costumes, and all the other children took their places, he saw a look of contentment spread its way across the music teacher's face.

She moved to the piano, where she didn't even bother to sit, and began the introductions to a few of the carols the children would sing during the course of the evening. The voices were simplistic in their singing, yet so noticeably graceful in their style. What a combination of clarity Celia had brought out in them with the natural gift of sound that had been planted in each child.

Then the six boy sopranos moved forward to begin the singing of *Gesu Bambino*. From the first words, "When blossoms flower'd mid the snows upon a winter night," the purity of their notes soared to the huge ceiling of the room. Brad was sure that when they went outside, there would be nothing stopping their angelic sounds from reaching all the way to the heavens.

It was not until then that Celia caught his eyes. She was gratified and humbled by the expression of admiration and appreciation that she saw in his face – the same look she had given him the evening before.

What a blessed holiday gift to find this brother in Christ, she mused, as she observed his love for the children that was as visible as her own.

When she had heard all that she wanted of the *Gesu Bambino*, and was sure that the students were ready for this evening of outreach she had planned for them, she stopped playing.

Dr. Lacey had come into the room to give his usual word of encouragement to the students. She allowed him his time, then called Brad to the piano beside her. The headmaster looked as surprised as the boys and girls to see the PE coach in this setting, much less asked to come and stand beside their cultural arts guru for the school. Celia could see the chaperoning teachers' heads turn toward each other.

She asked Brad, "Coach Simms," if he had any closing words for the students. Celia wished she could have made eye contact with each person in the room as she heard him say in a quiet tone, without the aid of his usual whistle hanging around his neck, "Let's bow for prayer."

Not another sound was heard as the person everyone perceived as "the jock" thanked God for the gift of each child, of their voices, their spirits, and the presents they had brought for a needy family.

"And Lord," Brad finished, "may these students know the joy of receiving more than they give, through the gift of themselves as they reach out to this family, to Donnie, Anna and Bobby."

At the conclusion of his prayer, Celia turned to the students, giving them the last of her carefully planned instructions. "The walk to the risers is going to symbolize our processional to Bethlehem. There are families on blankets sitting along the hillside, who have also come in costume to add to the authenticity of the event. Visitors will be winding their way up the long, sloping drive to experience this nativity setting first hand. They may stop. They may bring gifts. Whatever they do, I want you to remember that you are recreating a most blessed event, one that will impact this school and this community for a very long time, not only through the gifts that are given for Bobby this evening, but through the outpouring of love that will affect this precious child's entire life."

Both Dr. Lacey and Brad stood spellbound as Celia's words seemed to influence every person in the room, from the tenured teachers all the way to the youngest kindergarten children. It was rather like a voice coming from another source, one of God's own angels, telling everyone what was expected of him or her on this blessed and holy night. Awe seemed to be written on the face of each person standing around her.

Donnie and Anna had taken their places on the hillside beside the manger Art's father had purposely placed in a most auspicious spot. As Celia processed up the hill with the children and designated adults, she was completely overtaken by a feeling that absorbed her entire being. For what she saw as she looked at the couple, and watched Anna place Bobby in the manger, far surpassed anything she had imagined in her careful planning.

She sensed that the students felt the wonder, also, for they took their places on the risers with extreme caution. This was quite different from the other outdoor concerts where the boys usually pushed and shoved, clamoring to see who could get there first, and knocking off a couple of others on the way.

It was not until then that Celia noticed that cars lined the entire drive leading up to the school. Traffic was backed up on the highway as far as she could see over the hillside. And in the midst of it all, she saw uniformed policemen directing the through traffic, and that a lane had been designated for people attending the nativity and was lit with flares, giving the effect of luminaries all the way down the road.

She turned her head to look behind her, having an idea of whom the culprit was that instigated this most important factor that she had overlooked.

Brad and Dr. Lacey winked, simultaneously, at Celia. The PE coached mouthed the words, "It's a guy thing."

Celia gave him a thumbs-up sign, and an over enunciated, "Thanks," gratified that these two men had taken on a responsibility of their own for the school's project.

The smile on Brad's face showed his pride not only for himself, but for her, the students and the school as he jokingly mouthed back, "You can pay me later."

Determined not to let him have the last word, she returned, "You got it . . . at the Red Pig!" With that, Celia turned to sit on the bench before he had time to retaliate with another quip, knowing she would hear more later.

There was not a break in the spectators during the entire nativity, which lasted way past the planned two hours. Some people got out of their cars to get a closer look at Bobby and his parents. Children came and laid their families' gifts at the base of the manger. Cameras flashed throughout the evening. Newspaper reporters and television cameras tried to capture the essence of the live nativity in words and pictures.

It was obvious that people from all walks of life had come to participate in the support of the Little family. Men in construction clothes and muddy boots, women in heels and pearls, and children in ball uniforms all came to lay gifts at Bobby's feet.

The teacher was so proud of her students. Not once did they divert their attention away from their songs and her direction. She had tried to plan the music so that each group could watch the activities of the evening while other grade levels sang. She was more pleased that she didn't stare at the manger scene herself, given her fascination with this newly discovered family.

Then, like on cue, Celia noticed a restlessness in the students. She caught them focusing their attention toward the manger, so she likewise turned to see what was causing their stares.

There was a woman walking beside a young boy, both of whom looked as if they had appeared off the street, or from a homeless shelter. They had apparently walked here, which was in itself a major effort, given the academy's distance from the road, much less town.

Celia watched the young boy, dirty, and dressed in well-worn clothes, as he reached out to Anna and held a blanket up to her. The wrap had obviously been used - many times, in fact - for its edges were frayed and the fabric had holes from being held and laundered so much in the past.

The boy stood there, proud as a peacock, that he had given the baby a gift of love. He watched as Anna unfolded the blanket and wrapped it around Bobby, tucking it around her son to keep him warm.

The music teacher thought how perfect it was that the first and second graders were singing *The Friendly Beasts* in the background. She listened to the words which seemed so fitting, *"'I,' said the sheep with the curly horn, 'I gave him my wool for his blanket warm, he wore my coat on Christmas morn; I,' said the sheep with the curly horn."* Although the words of the carol were written in the twelfth century, they still held the same message for the children. As was usually the case, Celia was touched by the timeless beauty of words and music.

While the youngsters finished singing the carol, she heard one of the fourth grade girls whisper to her neighbor, "Ooh, germs."

Celia watched as a few of the girls began to squirm at the idea of that blanket touching their skin. A tiny smile broke across the teacher's face, for she secretly knew the love contained in that blanket far outweighed any germs that were on it.

The shepherds and the wisemen were getting audibly louder in their verbose argument of whose father had made the biggest donation, or given the best gift to the Little family.

Celia was about to flash her "stop that!" eyes over to them when she heard the little boy who had brought the blanket begin to speak. She watched as he looked up at his mother with huge, round eyes that themselves held a message of love.

He was still holding onto one of her hands, but with his other hand, the child reached up, tugged on her arm, and pulled her closer to his face.

Expecting him to whisper, Celia was surprised to hear him blurt out, "Mommy, they must not have ever heard Jesus' story about the rich man, and riding a camel through the eye of a needle."

His voice rang through the air, catching the attention of all the students. They looked at each other, their facial expressions clearly giving witness to which children knew that parable, and which did not.

Celia felt sure that before the evening was over, several of her flock would be looking up the scripture in the New Testament about the rich man, the camel, and the eye of a needle. *At least they'll learn one thing they'll never forget from this night.*

Smiling, she walked over to the little boy, knelt down and kissed his forehead. She was sure that he was the "real" angel of the evening, the same as the Angel of the Lord who came down to announce the birth of Christ. This young boy had truly been a messenger sent down from God to proclaim the truth of the blessedness of this baby that lay before all the "little rich kids."

Celia had wanted to give her students a lesson they would never forget. And as was the case with the baby Jesus, this young boy, also a child born into a poor, lowly estate, spoke to everyone in this community. She was sure that his gift had given her beloved children an example of giving that she could never have accomplished on her own.

Reporters had been scurrying to catch the boy's words, with cameramen clamoring to capture the scene, while the onlookers wiped tears from their eyes. Celia was certain that the late news would feature not one, but two poor families that had placed their mark on the town of Tillman and the hearts of all the families of its fine academy. She wished she could have caught Brad's face during the child's visit. But she was sure she would hear about everyone's reactions later.

The proud music teacher made her way slowly back to the keyboard. She took a long look at her students, gazing at each and every face. Her eyes, the same ones that had been full of burn-out only a few days ago, now beamed with the glow that came from a heart that had been "strangely warmed."

She motioned for one of her girls to move to the front of the students. The girl, who had been blessed with the voice of a songbird, was dressed in shabby attire – a loose, burlap dress dotted with several unmatched patches.

Celia began the introduction to the last song of the evening, the same song that had been the last one of the Christmas concert before the grand finale. Just as the *Gesu Bambino* had spoken to her on that evening, she was sure this song would speak to her now. Her heart that had been warmed was now ablaze with the Spirit that had filled her during the past several days. She prayed that the richness of the children's voices, concluded by the heaven-sent simplicity of this girl's solo on the last stanza, would touch the hearts, as her had been touched, of the crowd who had congregated to witness this special evening.

As she listened to the words of the final solo, *What can I give Him . . . give Him my heart*, there was no doubt in Celia's mind what the most meaningful gift of the evening had been. It was not the furniture, nor the donkeys and livestock, not the money, nor the clothes – not even the blanket. The gift that was sent from God, to another gift of God, was the poor young boy's example - the gift of his heart.

CHAPTER 10

When the last student had left, Celia walked back to her classroom to pack away all the costumes and instruments so that she, too, could go home and have a wonderful, and now extremely meaningful, *and "strangely warmed,"* holiday vacation. She was sure the gifts that poured in during the evening for Donnie, Anna and Bobby were only the beginning. The teacher fully expected endless offers would continue to pour in once word spread through the community about the needy family, and the live nativity the students had provided to help them.

Yes, word of mouth is the best advertisement, and this town is just small enough to have everyone talking. She smiled at the thought. *And of course, it will hit the Junior Charity League first.* Another grin. *It'll be interesting to see who has to out give whom with this.*

But as Celia had that thought, it saddened her that Bobby would receive some gifts that were only for show. She reflected on that, knowing they would be accepted with sincere gratitude, so from Donnie's standpoint, there would be no wrongdoing. The teacher only hoped he didn't know this social crowd as she did.

Yet, she determined, there has to be a charitable heart somewhere in all of these people, or they wouldn't give to anything. They would keep all of their wealth to themselves. *Or maybe not*, she reasoned, thinking of some of their charitable contributions as tax deductions, and an opportunity to take yet another write-off in the last few days of this year.

She decided this was not for her to worry over, for it did not concern her. But it *did* continue to fill her with a longing to instill in her students the art of giving. Thinking back over the night, Celia felt she had made a lot of headway toward the accomplishment of that goal.

As she closed the lid on the piano, she noticed a note in the recognizable, but barely readable, scribbling of Dr. Lacey. *Another thank-you note for a job well done!*

she smiled. Opening the envelope, she realized that she didn't need these personal accolades, but in a sense, she would miss their sentimental touch when she was no longer here.

This past week had definitely proven to Celia that she was to do more for people than sit on a bench for the rest of her life. She had no idea whether what she felt was the beginning of mid-life crisis, or the realization, like so many her age who were making desperate job changes, that she was missing out on her purpose in life. But for whatever reason, she knew that she wouldn't be in her present position when the next school year came.

Dear Celia, she read.

Hmm . . . that's strange. I've never known Dr. Lacey to start his notes with the word 'dear.' He usually just writes the first name and a short message - just enough to get the point across. I hope I haven't overstepped my boundaries by this act of kindness.

Celia continued to read, slowly, afraid of the words that might follow.

Congratulations on a job well done – as usual! You continually prove to be an asset to our fine establishment.

Please see me as soon as we come back from the holidays. On behalf of our Outreach Committee, I'd like to offer you the position as our new Director of Human Resources.

Of course, we can't let you completely out of the realm of music, so you will be the program director, and work with the boys' choir, and any other group of your choosing. We'll hire an assistant for the rest of your present responsibilities.

Think about this during the holidays, and if you're interested, let's sit down in January so that we can have the contract worked out before the end of February.

Sincerely,
George

The music teacher hadn't noticed her eyes watering until after she looked up from the note. She read it again to make sure this was not a dream, then sat down on the bench and began to play. Celia had no idea what she was playing, for her fingers, as usual, had a mind of their own as they glided across the notes of the melody that she subconsciously felt. She hummed the tune at first, trying to recognize in her head what was in her heart.

What can I give him, poor as I am? If I were a shepherd, I would bring a lamb. If I were a wise man, I would do my part. But what I can I give him: give him my heart.

Celia played the carol through again, singing the final stanza and hearing the words that had been sent to her from her own Angel of the Lord proclaiming the "good news." There was no doubt in her mind what her answer would be when she spoke with Dr. Lacey in January.

She placed the canvas cover over the piano, turned out the lights, and locked the door behind her. *Merry Christmas to all, and to all a good night*, she whispered as she took one last melancholic glance at the classroom, realizing that the next time she walked through that door, it would be a new year, *and* a new beginning.

"I began to wonder if you were going to spend Christmas here," she heard from a male voice in the hallway.

Celia grinned and turned toward the voice, gratified that Brad had taken the time to say farewell before leaving for his vacation. "I had to say good-bye to the place in my own way," she admitted.

"So I heard," Brad nodded. "That's why I didn't barge into your classroom. The music was beautiful. I enjoyed just listening to it."

"Music does have a way of speaking to me," she confessed.

Brad looked at the musician's face and hoped that he was not speaking out of turn. "Celia, I'm sure you read the note from Dr. Lacey and our outreach committee. I personally think you would be perfect for that position. Yet, music is such a strong part of your existence. Please don't give it up completely. You're too good at it."

She smiled appreciatively at his comment. "Thanks, Brad. I must admit, though, that's the last thing I expected to hear from a phys ed teacher."

"Yeah, I know. But I can't help it if I was blessed with good looks *and* a brain!"

Celia knew Brad was kidding with her, but she also knew that he'd been totally correct in his statement. And she wasn't about to comment on it further. If time opened that door down the road, so be it. But for now, that door needed to stay closed. She recognized that they both had some clear thinking to do before clouding their minds with anything personal. So she chose to roll her eyes at him, and give him nothing more than, "Yeah, yeah, yeah."

He reached out and took her hand. "Celia, my real reason for wanting to see you is to tell you that I'm going to visit my father on Christmas Day. I figured it's about time to bury the hatchet."

She took his other hand and turned to face him. Celia thought she caught the glint of a tear in his eye under the dim lights of the hallway.

He looked down into her eyes, allowing her to see that her vision was right. "Last night as we were talking, I was hoping to be the sounding board that you needed to help you come to terms about a long overdue resolution. A resolution between your mom and dad, your dad and you, your sister and your dad, and your sister and you."

Brad gently squeezed her fingers as he continued. "Then you made the comment about us taking things for granted, and not appreciating them when we have them. On my drive home, I kept thinking about that statement, for it said something totally different to me. It reminded me that we see things in others that we don't see in ourselves.

"I was so busy thinking about your resolution with your family that I didn't concentrate on the one I should have with my own father. Anyway, I laid awake for a good while last night thinking about how I need to make the first move with him. I have no idea how he will be, or if he will recognize me, or even know me. But I have to do this." There was a firm determination in his voice.

Celia didn't bother to tell Brad that her prayers from yesterday were working, too. It was then she realized that just as she had been unable to pray about her own situation, so had he with his. Their prayer partnership had a dual role, but she didn't feel the need to mention that now.

"I'm glad to hear you're going to see your father. I'll be thinking of you, and I'll be sure to say a special prayer."

"You do that."

The two teachers looked at each other, keenly

aware of the mutual friendship that was developing between them.

"Brad, thank you for all your help in getting ready for tonight . . . *and* for taking care of the traffic situation. You certainly made things a lot easier for me."

"It's me who should be thanking you. You've helped me to face a part of my life that I'd thrown aside for many years. There's something about Christmas that warms the soul."

"You can say *that* again," she noted, counting how many times she'd felt that "warm" feeling during the past week.

"Watching the children, and the baby, and your enthusiastic drive in doing something to make a difference in the lives of Donnie and Anna . . . well, it all spoke to me. After talking with you last night over dinner, I felt a tugging from years ago. A tugging that somehow made it seem possible to break the barrier between my father and myself. I only hope he can feel the same way when I see him."

"Me, too," Celia said, looking at the muscular man's wishful eyes. "But if it doesn't go as you hope, you've still chipped off the top of the iceberg." She tightened her grip on his hand. "That's the first, *and the biggest*, step."

Brad reached over and kissed the music teacher on the cheek, in the manner of a long-time friend. "Merry

Christmas, Celia."

"Merry Christmas to you, too, Brad. See you next year."

"You betcha," and he opened the front door and watched her go to her car before turning to go back toward the gym's parking lot.

Walking outside, she noticed that snowflakes were beginning to fall. The humbled teacher looked up in amazement. In all her life, she didn't remember a white Christmas in these parts. She had heard her mother talk about one the year Celia was a baby, but of course the teacher had no recollection of it. To see these flakes, it seemed a gift of nature, a perfect coda to the evening.

The large, frozen particles hit her face, sticking for a second before melting, lightly stinging, but still feeling wonderful. In all the night's excitement, she had failed to notice a drop in the temperature, and not one weather forecaster had predicted snow.

But then, Celia, that should have been a sure-fire sign it would happen, she grinned, remembering her grandmother's sideways comments to her meteorologist uncle, regarding his hit-and-miss forecasts.

It was a beautiful drive home through the countryside, with the rolling hills already turning white, as if a magnet were pulling the flakes together to form a warm blanket over the earth. The snow in itself was astounding, but the fact that it was sticking so quickly to the ground was even more miraculous.

Celia wondered about Donnie and Anna and the baby. Then she realized that they had plenty of heat to keep them warm, as she thought of their surprise at returning to a cabin full of light and warmth, *and a TV*. The one who had provided this winter wonderland had surely protected that blessed family. She chose not to worry any more about them, knowing there was no way she could pry them from their home on this particular evening.

Nor should I even if I could, she mused, comparing the parallels of this modern-day family to Mary and Joseph and the baby Jesus.

CHAPTER 11

The snowflakes only served to revitalize the tired teacher. Feeling that her Christmas vacation could now officially begin, Celia went home and prepared for a long, relaxing evening rather than going to bed as she had planned.

She walked in the door, full of an awe that had been brought on by all the happenings of the evening. She had heard the Christmas story read multiple times over the past thirty-seven years of her life. But tonight, Celia had *lived* the Christmas story. She had seen throngs of people come, bearing gifts, for a baby for which they had only heard about from her "angels" - her students - who had gone home and told their families and friends and neighbors "all they had seen and heard."

Over the years, Celia had seen children come to life as characters once they put on costumes and got on the stage. But tonight was beyond belief. And to think they had been sent their own "Angel of the Lord," in the form of a young boy, who taught the students a lesson she could never have gotten across to them.

Her prayer to the Light, on that evening a couple of nights ago while rocking Bobby, had certainly been heard. *Not only heard, but answered.*

The tired teacher moved to her bedroom, where she changed into her comfy old, pink chenille robe and worn slippers. Then she walked quietly into the kitchen and put on some water to boil. After turning on the gas logs, she picked up her new holiday novel from the end table and sat back in her winged chair beside the fireplace.

It seemed strange that she was finally getting to start what she had planned to do three evenings ago, but tonight, there was something special, even to the point of being sanctimonious, about the evening.

Celia opened the pages that she had tried to start reading then, but had held no meaning. Once again, her mind stopped her. She glanced up at the clock on the mantle, the same one that had been announcing the time to her family for several decades, as it chimed twelve bells. It was Christmas Eve. She was a teacher of children. A major tradition for years had been to read the Christmas story, and the poem by Clements. This year, she'd not had time to think about that poem.

She went back to the kitchen, poured a cup of chocolate, and returned to the living room. Celia sat back, relaxing, with her head resting against the high back of the chair. In her mind she recited, "Twas the night before Christmas and all through the house, not a creature was stirring, not even a mouse."

The words stopped. Celia could envision the log cabin, the rust on the tin roof glowing in the moonlight, and snow on the ground. She was sure that even the mice were keeping watch over the young child on this night, filled with wonder that such a small being could make such a difference. And she could imagine the doe she had seen at the edge of the trees on that first evening, joined by the donkey that Art's dad had moved to the farm, and ducks from the pond, looking toward the house, listening intently to the tender cry of the new-born baby, ready to share their hay or whatever they had, just like the friendly beasts of the carol by the same name. Red cardinals were surely perched on the branches of the nearby holly trees, their feathers matching the brightness of the berries, next to the ivy that ran across the ground near the trees and along the rock wall in front of the cabin.

A smile spread across Celia's face. The Light was shining down on the cabin this night. *This night and every night.*

The ringing of the phone dissolved her image of the home of country bliss. She reached for the receiver, wondering who would be calling at this time of night.

"Miss Brinkley, this is Durant Ridenhour. I hope I didn't wake you."

Lane's father, the banker. He must have a monetary report for me on how much they collected for Bobby and his family. "Oh, no. I haven't been home long."

"Good. I apologize for calling so late, but I assumed you would still be up after the big night you had. I knew you couldn't have been home for too long by the time you finally got to leave the school. I have some great news for you - news I felt couldn't wait until school started back, and news I felt might make your Christmas merrier.

"The total of money raised tonight at the nativity scene was $28, 963.00."

Celia closed her eyes, held her head back and felt her heart skip a beat. She listened intently to the rest of Mr. Ridenhour's words.

"Sid Barber, who is Drew's dad, and I added enough to round that off to $30,000.00, and we've gotten pledges from five of the national corporations in our county to double that amount.

And just before I called you, I got a call from Dale Jarrett's business manager. The Nascar driver and Dale Jarrett Ford are donating a new car to the Little's. "

The teacher was so ecstatic she fell into the chair, barely able to listen to his next words.

"Celia Brinkley, you should be very proud of yourself. With the donations you had already accumulated, you've raised over $100,000.00 for this needy family."

The teacher took a deep breath, wondering if she could even speak for the fluttering of her heart.

"No, Mr. Ridenhour, these students and this community raised $100,000.00 for this needy family. I only sat back quietly and heard God's voice."

"Well, that must have been some pretty loud voice because this is quite an accomplishment."

"Yes, I guess you could say that," she grinned, wishing Brad could have heard this news. "That same voice has been telling me a lot lately, all of it loudly enough to catch my attention."

The banker continued in his jovial, yet professional tone. "The bank is closed until the 27th with the holiday falling on the weekend the way it does. I'll get with Sid and we'll get this set up in some sort of trust, or let you tell us exactly how we need to work it so that the family can get the place fixed up to standards, then put the rest aside for the baby.

"Fortunately, I've found out that our bank holds the mortgage on the Little's house, so I'm going to look into some options that may make the payments a little more bearable for them. I'm not making any promises on that end, but I'll certainly see if there's anything we can do to help."

"Thank you, Mr. Ridenhour. Thank you for everything. And thank you for calling. This is the most wonderful Christmas gift anyone could have given me." She paused for a moment, stopping the tears of joy that were trying to make their way into the conversation. "May I share this information with the media?"

"Absolutely. They helped make this possible, and I feel, as I'm sure you do, that the community has a right to know the fruits of their labor."

"Or giving, as the case may be," Celia chuckled, adding the first light moment of the serious conversation.

"Right you are."

The teacher, now beaming with pride at the accomplishment of her students, heard a break in the business tone of the banker's voice.

"Good night, Miss Brinkley. And a Merry Christmas."

"A Merry Christmas to you and your family, too,

Mr. Ridenhour. May your children get everything they want from Santa."

Celia hung up the phone knowing that her last statement was a given, the same as it would be for every other family of Tillman Academy. But that was alright. For in their giving, they had all reached out and helped someone in need. They had made Christmas merry for another, one less fortunate than themselves. Perhaps they had not given until it hurt, but they had given. They had learned a valuable lesson, and this was a wonderful beginning for them.

How proud she was as she retreated back to her chair beside the fireplace, and how she wished she could call someone and share the news.

Oh well, I know what will be the topic of discussion at my family's Christmas dinner, she thought, looking forward to the wonderful dinners she would share with her parents and family over the next couple of days. In a little over twelve hours, she would be sitting down to dine with them for the first of several meals.

Celia truly *was* looking forward to the time she would have to spend with all of them this holiday season. And for some *known* reason, she was even excited about getting down on the floor and playing with all the nieces and nephews.

She opened her novel for a third time and read the first page aloud, taking a big sip of hot chocolate filled with cinnamon, and becoming completely engrossed in the story. The sound of voices of the boys' ensemble singing *Gesu Bambino* floated in her head as she turned the pages.

Those boys who had first been a part of her experience of feeling "strangely warmed." Those boys who had gotten into a verbal boasting war over whose father had given the baby the most. Those boys who had all learned a new Bible story this night. And most importantly, those boys who would never forget dressing in costume to pay tribute to a child born into the world, void of all the excessive material gifts to which they had each been privy.

As she sat reading, Celia prayed that those boys had reaped something, something very valuable, from this night. She prayed that they would each, sometime in their own lives, feel that sensation of being "strangely warmed."

Recalling the intensity of emotion she felt at that moment during the concert, a feeling that was truly divinely inspired, the humbled teacher sensed that it was a part of her calling. A calling that was going to take her from the classroom to a position of reaching out to others in a new and different way. And a calling that was going to allow her to teach the students many more important lessons, lessons for life, than anything she had ever done during her music classes with them.

She felt that her new career was going to allow her to work with those same students, the ones she loved so much, her own children. God had given her a very special gift this holiday, and in so doing, He had allowed her to give a gift, an extremely extraordinary gift, to those students. Now she was going to return that gift by giving of herself to the One who had so richly blessed her.

Celia closed her eyes and envisioned those six boys in their robes of the shepherds and the wisemen. Their unadulterated voices filled the room as she allowed her memory to take shape, hearing the girl's solo voice in the background. *What can I give him, poor as I am? If I were a shepherd, I would bring a lamb. If I were a wise man, I would do my part. Yet what I can I give him: give my heart.*

The teacher was sure she would never forget the image of those boys. Not the night on the stage when they were a part of the most wonderful feeling she had ever experienced in her entire life, or tonight, dressed in costume, when they had given her an insight into her future. Little did they know they had given *her* the best lesson of all.

A look of satisfaction spread over Celia's face as she recalled that soft low cry of Bobby as those boys produced the purest of tones, the notes floating across the air on a single syllable, "*Ah - - -,*" then finishing with, "*O come, let us adore Him.*"

CHAPTER 12

Anna rocked her baby in the chair that had belonged to the child's great-great-grand-father. She had frequently wondered if the saints in heaven were able to look down upon their loved ones on the earth. Although she still had no definite answer for that question, she felt that at the moment, the ances-tors from the previous four generations were smiling down on this infant, their descendant, from heaven. If they weren't, at least God was. There was no doubt in her mind, as she saw the glow around Bobby's face, that he was blessed.

And so are your father and I, she whispered, as if the child knew exactly what she was saying.

She thought back over the events of the past few days and how different their lives were from what they had been only hours ago. There was absolutely no explanation for the way things had transpired other than the fact that some power, an Omnipotent Power, was touching them with His hand.

The mother suddenly felt completely overwhelmed. She and Donnie had known that they would be alright, that things would work out for them and their precious firstborn. They had not been anxious, only trusting and faithful with their prayers and their determination to keep the farm in the family at all costs.

Now it looked as if their dreams were all coming true. Anna wanted to pinch herself to make sure that all this had really happened and that she was not in a dream, caught up by all the emotions of the special holiday and all the recent happenings. Yet as she looked around the room, and felt the warmth of heat that they hadn't known so far this winter season, she knew that the dream was indeed reality.

When they had turned into the driveway, all the lights in the small cabin were on, and the house was filled with heat, rather than just having a few candles and one spot of warmth from the woodstove. A television was set up in front of the sofa, ready to show the late news and Bobby. How in the world Celia Brinkley had been able to pull off all the miracles of the evening was beyond her, but Anna knew there was only one explanation. The same Omnipotent Power that had blessed them was obviously very much at work in the life of the music teacher.

And how unfortunate that Miss Brinkley had shared with her, only a couple of days before in the classroom, how she intended to change jobs by the beginning of the next school year. The school would be deeply saddened by that loss. They might find another who was as professionally adept as their current teacher, but they would be greatly challenged in finding another person with her talents and her love for people, especially all those children.

Anna's mind turned to the children who had sung to Bobby the day of Celia's last music class before the holiday. Those voices were still audible in her head. She heard the rich tones of *Away in a Manger* as she took the baby to the crib and laid him in front of the window.

Amazement and wonder filled her heart as Anna noticed that the candle in the window had been replaced with a battery-operated one. She wound the mobile that Celia had brought two evenings ago, and watched the animals turn as the music played. It thrilled her to see Bobby's tiny head turn toward the melody he heard.

The mother looked at the crèche set in the window.

It was then that she noticed the animals outside the window looking in, as if taking in the sound of the mobile and the sight of the nativity set, while themselves keeping watch over her own child. Anna knew that she was privy to a living miracle, happening right in front of her very eyes.

She closed her eyes and listened to the children's voices in her head as they sang the same words she heard in her prayer for the baby. *Be near me Lord Jesus, I ask thee to stay close by me forever, and love me, I pray. Bless all the dear children in thy tender care, and fit us for heaven to live with thee there. Amen*, the mother whispered as she bent and softly kissed Bobby on the cheek.

Standing up, she noticed Donnie by the corner of the house looking up at the evening sky. She wondered what thoughts must be running through his head, and what pride must be in his heart and soul at the reality that he was going to be able to hold onto this farm.

Anna turned and went to the kitchen, fixing their last cup of coffee on the old wooden stove. Their new appliances would be delivered in the morning, even though it would be Christmas Eve. The students' families had gone way beyond the call of outreach to make sure that Donnie and she had the perfect holiday with their son.

As much as she was once again looking forward

to the convenience of modern technology, she knew she would miss the lessons she'd learned in these past few months. They had served her well, as Anna knew they had Donnie.

She closed her eyes again, praying they wouldn't lose sight of their family's humble beginnings in this cabin. Looking back in on the baby, she realized they would not, for every time they saw that precious gift God had given them, the sight of this place, as it was now, would again take shape in their minds.

Anna poured two cups of hot coffee and sat down at the old piece of plywood atop the sawhorses for the last time, finishing the prayer she had started moments earlier.

I love thee, Lord Jesus, look down from the sky, and stay by my cradle till morning is nigh.

❄ ❄ ❄

Filling the animals' troughs with hay and feed, Donnie stood thinking of the scene on the evening Jesus had been born. He took in the smells, the sights, and the sounds of the barn and the nearby animals, letting them waft him away to that night long ago.

Here, in their poor state, he and Anna were blessed with a place to lay Bobby besides a lowly manger in a grotto on the side of a hill. And like all parents, the gift of their baby boy was a blessing from above. But somehow, through all the events that had transpired over the past few days, and especially on this night, he felt a parallel to that first night of wonder.

How amazed and humbled Mary and Joseph must have felt. Yet how proud they must have been to be the parents of a tiny child who caused such a stir among all the townspeople, and even brought in rich guests from afar. And how odd some of the gifts of honor, gifts fit for a king, must have seemed to them in their simple lifestyle.

Donnie took in a deep breath of the cold night air and let it out slowly, allowing it to be a part of all the sensual perception he was experiencing. The snow that had begun on the way home from the school was continuing to fall, covering the ground so that his footprints and the hoof prints of the animals showed under the light from the sky. It seemed strange that the moon was still shining, full in its shape and casting a majestic brightness on a cloudy evening that bore frozen droplets from heaven.

He noticed the animals moving toward the cabin, as if caught up in the wonder of what had happened this evening, and they, too, were coming to pay homage to his dear son. Words to the carol he had heard the children sing in Miss Brinkley's classroom filled his head. *The cattle are lowing, the baby awakes, but little Lord*

Jesus, no crying he makes.

The proud father noticed that the clouds had broken a bit and in the small clearings between them, a few stars peeked through, trying to get a glimpse of all that was going on below them. His mind continued to sing, *the stars in the sky looked down where he lay, the little Lord Jesus asleep on the hay.*

As the sky took on the color of a deep, blue velvet, the stars and the moon began to take precedence over the clouds as the snow lessened to only a few flakes, still finding their way to the earth.

He stared into the sky, wondering if it, too, held any likeness to the evening of Jesus' birth. Suddenly, a star shot across the sky, a white tail trailing behind it, giving it the appearance of an angel taking flight from the heavens to someone in need down below.

The simple man, who now felt like the richest man on the face of the earth, quickly made a wish - a wish that through his son's life, God's will would come to pass.

What an evening this had been. What a lesson he had learned. What a lesson the children had learned. And how God had blessed every soul who had been a part of the evening.

Donnie couldn't help but wonder how Celia Brinkley must feel, having been the instigator, the mastermind, of the event that had brought an entire town together. However, staring up at the sky as he walked back toward the house, he realized that she was not the one who had ordained this night. She had only seen the Light.

He remembered the teacher's words from the night of the concert, when she described hearing a baby's low cry during the boys' singing of *Gesu Bambino*. "Strangely warmed," she had called it.

Donnie knew exactly what she meant. For now he, too, was filled with all that the Almighty had created, and done, and ordained, and blessed, and how He had allowed so many people to come together and share in His love. He began to wonder how many of the guests had any idea of the impact of the gift they had also received on this evening.

Before going back inside, he knelt on the front steps, in front of the animals that had gathered there, and offered a prayer to the baby's *real* father, the Father of all who had come to Tillman Academy this night.

❄ ❄ ❄

Donnie rested his head on the pillow, tired from all the academy's events of the past few weeks, but wide awake from the excitement of the evening. He turned his head to look at Anna, who was already sound asleep. Then he looked over toward the crib, with the nativity set in the window behind it. He could still picture the boys who had worn the shepherds' and kings' robes that evening. The words to the last verse of the poem by Christina Rosetti, the same carol the young girl sang, echoed through his head. *What can I give him, poor as I am? If I were a shepherd, I would bring a lamb. If I were a wise man, I would do my part. Yet what I can I give him: give my heart.*

And from somewhere off in the distance, like a soft lullaby coming from just over the hillside, he heard bells chiming the music that he had heard the children singing only nights before. He closed his eyes and imagined soft white flakes of snow falling while he quietly huumed the music he was hearing in his head, of the evening that spoke to him, *in the bleak midwinter.*

In the Bleak Midwinter

In the bleak midwinter, frosty wind made moan,
earth stood hard as iron, water like a stone;
snow had fallen, snow on snow, snow on snow,
in the bleak midwinter, long ago.

Our God, heaven cannot hold him, nor earth sustain,
heaven and earth shall flee away when he comes to reign.
In the bleak midwinter a stable place sufficed
the Lord God Almighty, Jesus Christ.

Angels and archangels may have gathered there,
cherubim and seraphim thronged the air;
but his mother only, in her maiden bliss,
worshiped the beloved with a kiss.

What can I give him, poor as I am?
If I were a shepherd, I would bring a lamb;
if I were a Wise Man, I would do my part;
yet what I can I give him: give my heart.

~ Christina G. Rosetti ~

About the Artist

RuthEllen Busbee-Boerman discovered her God-given talent for painting in 1983, while helping her son with a school project. After appearing at art festivals and craft shows, and experiencing an emotionally trying time and "burn-out", she felt God was molding her to become a Christian artist.

With the success of her most popular print, *The True Vine*, RuthEllen was sure the Lord wanted her to devote the majority of her time to Christian art. Almost all of her paintings contain hidden religious objects or symbols, and most carry a spiritual message.

Mrs. Boerman is currently painting a series of twelve paintings based on the 23rd Psalm, and *The True Vine II*. She also does commissioned works of homes and country scenes.

Ruth Ellen, of Hendersonville, NC, is available for a limited number of appearances each year.

About the Author

_____

Catherine Ritch Guess, also a published composer, is presently working on a recording to go with each of her book titles. After serving as an Organist/Minister of Music for over three decades, she now spends her time writing, speaking or performing for a variety of venues.

Guess, who holds degrees in Church Music, Music Ed and a Master's Degree in Christian Education, is a Diaconal Minister of the United Methodist Church, currently appointed as the Circuit Riding Musician.

Catherine is busy completing a sequel to this book, *There's a Song in the Air,* and an Easter novel, *The Old Rugged Cross.*